IAN WOODHEAD

UPWORLD

SEVERED PRESS
HOBART TASMANIA

UPWORLD

PROLOGUE

South America 1968

Vincent Delano slammed his hand across his sweat-slicked mouth to stop the panicked shriek from blasting through the dense jungle. Oh God, one of those monsters had reached Frederico already! The blood, it had to be *the blood*. The sound of those terrible claws digging through the loose soil made him want to weep. Why had he gone to all the trouble of dropping him into that pit in the first place?

He peered around the edge of the towering black monolith and fearfully gazed back along the path that he had cut through the jungle while fleeing from his crime.

The last of his companions screamed out his last breath. The jungle around him had now fallen silent, as if they, like Vincent, didn't want that vicious giant creature that shouldn't even exist, to know that other prey still remained.

He forced hot jungle air into his burning lungs, while he listened to that thing tear into Frederico's body. There was no need to panic now, Vincent could scale down the anxiety. After all, despite everything that this place had thrown at him, he was safe now. He had passed across the markers. That monster wouldn't be following him in here.

They told Vincent that no jungle creature would enter the forbidden zone.

He opened his mouth and drew in a lungful of hot jungle air, while he pressed his body against the smooth stone in an attempt to stem the shakes that spread through his body. He almost dropped his revolver onto the stone floor.

Poor Frederico. He had been a good companion and colleague.

His faithful servant did not deserve such a brutal death, that's for sure. The man certainly didn't deserve his master to turn on him and shoot the poor man in the foot.

He opened the chamber and peered through the five holes. One bullet left. If Vincent had been thinking straight, he would have just buried the machete into Frederico's leg, instead of wasting valuable ammunition.

Vincent composed himself. Luckily, there was nobody left to witness him losing control. He snapped the gun shut. To think that, not two minutes ago, he was actually contemplating using that last bullet on himself. To think that he, the greatest explorer in the western world, had sunk so low to have even considered taking his own life. Vincent was almost ashamed of himself.

A terrible squawking sound burst from beyond the foliage. He swallowed hard. The monster was no longer alone. The others had joined it to share the food, just as he predicted.

"It was a great sacrifice you made, Frederico," he whispered.

He crouched and pushed his hand into his tattered satchel and pulled out his treasured binoculars. It pleased him greatly that these had survived unscathed. Vincent had lost every member of his expedition to the monsters. They had picked them off one by one, just like that tribal elder had foreseen. Still, they could be replaced. His binoculars on the other hand? Vincent would had been heartbroken if anything had happened to these.

These had belonged to his grandfather. The old man told Vincent that he had ripped these from the neck of a German sniper. The dirty bastard had shot at the brave infantry captain and missed. The German had tried and failed to shoot again, but his grandfather was faster. Even while the battle raged on, with artillery shells raining down around them, the captain and climbed out of the trenches and charged the German's position. He stood there, a prime target for the enemy machine gun emplacements. He took aim and shot the sniper in the head.

Vincent was so proud to come from a family line of heroes and could now state that he too was a hero, just like his grandfather. After all, there was nobody else on this planet who could say they had survived several vicious attacks from a flock of giant, nine-foot-tall, prehistoric flesh-eating birds.

He adjusted the settings while grinning at the noise of fighting reaching his ears. Good, while they were busy arguing over the remaining bloodied chunks of Frederico, it would give him a little more time to put some more distance between him and them.

He still wasn't totally convinced that this so-called sacred area would keep them out. He should already be on his way, but Vincent still needed evidence. A couple of photographs would prove they really do exist.

The view showed him nothing but leaves. They were there, in the clearing, making enough noise to wake the dead, but neither of them was going to show their ugly faces anytime soon. Vincent then caught a glimpse of bright blue plumage through the greenery. He was almost tempted to move forward, right up to the wooden stake which marked the boundary and make some noise himself, but caution got the better of him.

Now that he knew they existed, Vincent could return, this time with a more experienced team; a group of men who actually knew what they were doing. He pushed the binoculars back into the satchel and stood, brushing off a couple of insects that were crawling up his dark green trousers.

So much for the forbidden zone stopping bugs.

"Stupid superstitious rubbish," he murmured as he made his way back to the huge monolith. Vincent tapped his forefinger on the smooth surface. Obviously not all of what the local tribesmen had told him was based on superstition. Those guardians who'd just eaten his entire group had shown him that.

So, if the giant terror birds were real, then the fabled city of the *First People* must exist as well. Of course it existed, why else would these magnificent stones be here if it wasn't true? Not that he needed any sub-human, dirty primitive to tell him something he already knew. Vincent had been searching for the First People for over twenty years. For over two decades, the scientific community scorned his work and laughed at his notions of an advanced culture that predated the Mesoamerican civilisations by thousands of years. Not that any of them laugh in front of him, *they wouldn't dare*, the spineless fools. He would show those cretins; he would show all of them that he was right all along.

Vincent ran his fingers along the stone. *This must mark its boundary*. As far as he was concerned, its discovery, as well as all its secrets and treasure, was within his grasp. He was about to become the most famous man on the planet.

He slung the satchel over his shoulder, picked up his machete, and started the slow process of hacking through more of the undergrowth. Even over the sound of his razor-sharp blade slicing through the vegetation, the noise of the giant birds still bickering over their meal reached his ears. Considering the size of the things, he would have thought they would have finished off the servant by now.

Then again, they probably weren't used to eating so much rich food in one day. As he cut through a vine as thick as his ankle, Vincent realised that if he was as cautious as he kept telling himself, all the other members of this expeditionary group might still be alive.

***

After three long days in this blasted oppressive hell hole, Vincent Delano's patience had worn down to almost nothing. He sat in his cotton-covered chair, sipping the last of the single malt, while having to listen to those lazy idiots' mumble under their breath about not eating since yesterday.

Vincent took out a strip of beef jerky and bit off the end. He'd never been with a more workshy bunch of bone-idle clowns in all his life. They were supposed to be taking down their tents in readiness to move out, but you could be sure that as custard is yellow, none of them would have gotten off their dead behinds to do anything but smoke. Vincent chewed on the meat. If they thought he was going to pay them for their shameful performance, then they had another thing coming. He wasn't going to pay them anyway, not after the disgraceful way they have spoken to him. Granted, they had muttered the insults under their breath and in a different language, but that wasn't the point. Vincent had excellent hearing. He was also fluent in over a dozen languages.

He would have confiscated their supplies if the greedy, thoughtless bastards hadn't already ploughed their way through the dried fruit and bread he had generously given them. Wasn't it convenient that those fools never ran out of tobacco? He wouldn't be at all surprised if the servants hadn't swapped some of their food supplies for native tobacco back at their last stop.

"God damn savages," he said to himself.

Vincent had enough supplies to keep him going for another two days. After the single malt, the cigars, and jerky went, he would just have to radio for Desmond to bring the helicopter from the main base back on the edge of Manaus.

It wouldn't come to that, this time. Vincent was sure the Gods would reward his persistence. All he wanted was some sign that he was at least heading in the right direction and on the right track. Was that really too much to ask for?

It was getting to the point where he was even beginning to doubt his own convictions. This was his seventh trip out into the middle of the Amazon in a decade. If Vincent didn't come back with some tangible proof this time, it's probable that the trust wouldn't fund another trip, no matter how much he protested.

Vincent sighed loudly. He drained his glass before he stuck his head through the tent flap. All the servants suddenly made it look as though they had lots of work to do. Just as he suspected, they had only just started on taking down their tents. If he had his way, he would beat them all with a thin stick. Vincent wasn't allowed to do that anymore. Still, his manic glare did give those layabouts something to think about.

The only one not pretending to work was his favourite servant, Frederico, and that's because he sent him along to scout the area north of the campsite. Vincent's one saving grace in this whole sordid affair had been a fortuitous encounter with a small tribe of natives two days ago. They, like many of the others in this area, had already been contaminated by western influences. This one even knew about Vincent's hunt for the mythical First People. The chief even claimed to possess one of their skulls.

Those smarmy savages didn't get the better of him, oh no. Vincent saw a con trick when he knew one. He ignored the protests from his servants and the objections from the elder, walking right up to the old man's raised chair inside his hut and pulled the skull from its mountings.

After all the theatre, it turned out to be a skull belonging to some long-dead gorilla. Quite how the skull of an African primate ended up in the middle of the Amazon jungle was a question he'd posed to the tribal elder. Of course, it was at that point when the greasy little man suddenly decided that he'd forgotten how to speak. That little oversight was soon corrected when Vincent pushed the nuzzle of his revolver against the head of a pretty little girl, who just so happened to be one of the chief's favourite daughters.

A torrent of insults spewed from the chief's mouth, as well as a name, *zona proibida,* The Forbidden Zone. Vincent had almost laughed. How stupid did they think he was? That sounded like something straight from a crappy B movie. It wasn't until he realised that the old man wasn't putting it on. He knew genuine fear when he saw it. Also, wasn't Vincent's reaction very similar to how the rest of the scientific community treated him back home?

He finished off his beef jerky while watching the sun break through the jungle canopy. He had sent Frederico off to check it out, while he got the camp ready to move. He locked away his belongings, grabbed his satchel, and instructed the others to start disassembling his tent. He left the idiots and set off to find what was taking Frederico so long, hoping the other servants wouldn't break any of his gear or steal any of his food.

Vincent found the servant an hour later, standing on the edge of the deep ravine, looking down into the valley below. Frederico didn't answer any of Vincent's calls. He didn't even turn around. When he reached the motionless man, Vincent saw exactly why the servant was paralysed with fear. He had found the tribe's *zona proibida* and the reason as to why this area of jungle terrified the natives.

Frederico was mumbling two words under his breath over and over: *pássaros demoníaco.* Demon birds.

Vincent had discovered a species of animal thought to have died out long before man had ever set foot on this continent. Streaking across the grasslands, a hundred foot below, were a dozen carnivorous flightless birds. The smallest one was easily a foot taller than him. They were running down a Pampas deer.

He sat down and watched in fascination as these magnificent creatures formed a horseshoe around the deer, boxing it in, before the animal in the middle let out an ear-piercing shriek. It charged forward and brought its massive head down, its heavy beak smashing into the deer's spine.

In the distance, poking through the greenery, Vincent saw the remains of some kind of wide towers built from black stone. That alone warranted further investigation. He knew for a fact that there should be no Mesoamerican structures in this part of the region. At least, none recorded.

Vincent ordered the servant back to the camp and told him to bring the others, and their equipment. He couldn't help grinning. After all those years, he had finally found the lost city of the First People. A race of legendary giant humanoid beings lost in the midst of time.

It took a couple of kicks to get Frederico moving. Once the servant had left him, Vincent settled down to watch the giant birds eat their kill.

***

Looking back, Vincent thought perhaps it might have been a better idea to wait for more back up, to have called for the helicopter. Entering this place with those incompetent fools had been asking for trouble. They never stood a chance against those feathered predators. None of them listened to his commands. If they had, then at least some of them might have lived.

Vincent wished a couple of those idiots hadn't ended up inside those giant turkeys. It would have meant that they'd be the ones hacking through this bloody jungle. This was tiring work, certainly not something that an eminent archaeologist should be doing.

He cut through another thick vine and stopped to mop his brow. No, he couldn't call for back-up, no way, not until he was absolutely sure that the lost city was here. Vincent knew there were spies amongst his people. He'd known that for years.

He had also suspected that The Trust already had prior knowledge of the giants long before he had become convinced of their existence. Why else would they so readily agree to his request for funding, over and over, despite his failures?

The Trust played the long game, and their patience had won out in the end. A find like this could even guarantee a place within the shadowy organisation's inner council. That alone was worth having to go through watching those terror birds tear up his team. A place in The Trust's inner council meant that he'd have unrestricted access to all of their libraries and the hidden museums. It's even rumoured that their collections made the antiquities stashed away under Vatican City look like the contents of some poor child's toy box.

Vincent Delano wasn't the only fringe academic employed by the shadowy organisation. He personally knew of two other archaeologists currently seeking the same prize as him. They were the ones who would have inserted spies into his camp. If they found out exactly how close he was, those bastards would take over, only after making sure that he disappeared first.

His continued hacking rewarded Vincent with another small clearing. He pushed his way through the gap he'd created. He put the machete back in the shear and used his thumbs to massage the small of his back. This was no natural clearing. He rubbed the soul of his boot across the jungle floor and grinned one more time when his rubbing exposed grey stone.

He dropped to his knees and cleared away as much debris as he could, each wipe, showing Vincent more of the flat, smooth stone. His heart thudded against his ribs when his excavations uncovered something that wasn't grey stone. He stopped his exertions and gazed down at the thin green vines which had grown around something that certainly wasn't natural. His mouth dried up as he carefully unthreaded two strands of plant material, exposing more of the golden metal.

Vincent stopped. He reached into his satchel and brought out his camera. This needed recording before excitement got the better of him. He stood and took a picture of the object's surroundings before he knelt back down and took another picture of the half-uncovered object. Only then did he carefully remove the rest of the vegetation from his find.

He stared at it for a full minute before taking one more picture.

Vincent had found the first definite proof that the First People really did exist. He dug out his well-thumbed notepad and eagerly flipped to near the end of the book, searching for a drawing he'd sketched on one of the first digs just after the end of the war. *There it was.* The picture of what was claimed to be a harmonic blade. A device that the First People used to create their fabulous city.

He carefully picked it up and turned the golden artefact around. It was shaped like a knife. He guessed that most people would even believe that was what this was. He, on the other hand, knew better. Vincent compared the real thing to the drawing he had made all those years ago. It was almost exact. He held the device in his hand, unable to wrap his fingers around the thick cylindrical handle. It was easily as thick as the metal mug that Frederico used to use to drink that vile coffee of his. There was a diamond-shaped indentation on the base of the knife. That was where they used to push in the power source, a green crystal. According to what he'd read, when this blade was activated, it would cut through anything solid.

He wrapped the blade in some old cloth and placed it at the bottom of his satchel before standing. Did he have enough evidence to present to The Trust to ask for funding for another expedition? Vincent decided to press on, believing that as soon as the helicopter pilot saw those giant birds, the discovery would spread like wildfire. It's highly likely that his enemies would get Trust funding meant for him before he even made it back.

Vincent slowly got to his feet. There wasn't a chance that he would allow anyone else to steal this discovery away from him. He had put in too many years of hard work to allow that to happen. This belonged to him alone.

He walked the perimeter of the clearing and found disappointment sinking in once again. He saw nothing beyond this clearing, which pointed to more evidence that some ancient civilisation once lived close by. Vincent turned to face the hole he had made. Even though he wasn't far from the boundary of this forbidden zone, the jungle had already swallowed up those monoliths. Vincent could be just metres away from more evidence of their presence, but thanks to all this vegetation, he could walk right past it without noticing. Maybe he should ring this in after all?

With a larger, more experienced team, Vincent would make short work of clearing this area. If anything was hidden under all this growth, he would uncover it. He returned to where he found the blade and sat down. The existence of the terror birds alone should be enough for The Trust to believe that Vincent was more than capable of doing this. Once he showed them the blade, well, he just knew that they'd give him anything he cared to ask for.

Time was no longer on his side either. It wouldn't be long before darkness crept in, and Vincent had no intentions of staying here until dawn. He rubbed away some more of the vegetation until the tip of his finger found a long, straight groove. He got onto his knees and crawled along the floor, following the groove, and brushing away the green as he advanced. The groove turned left ninety degrees just before he reached the edge of the clearing. His heartbeat notched up again when he believed he might have found his way inside.

He spent another twenty minutes clearing away the vegetation, grinning wider and wider each time the groove turned another ninety degrees. Vincent found himself back where he started, after exposing a square groove, twice the length of him.

Standing, he turned around, and clambered up one of the smaller trees. From this position, he could clearly see another oddity exactly in the middle of the square. The ground was raised a few inches. He jumped down and hurried into the middle. He dropped on his knees and brushed away the vines and leaves, discovering a thick block of black stone. Unlike the rest of the material that he'd uncovered, this block wasn't smooth. Writing of some type had been carved into all five sides of the stone. He leaned closer and attempted to dig out some of the mud from one of the shapes.

The failing light made it difficult to make out the exact shape. Even if the sun was on his side, Vincent doubted that he'd be able to decipher the inscriptions. He took another couple of pictures, before once more, wondering if he should leave. The light was failing faster than he anticipated. Again, he swore at his team for getting themselves killed. If those idiots were still alive, they would have been able to stay right here.

It was no good; Vincent would just have to call for the back-up before it got too dark to see. Did terror birds roost at night? If they did, then the chopper might not see them, meaning his discovery would be safe. After all, it's not like there was anybody else left alive to open their big mouths.

Vincent grinned to himself. He'd just have to say that his team had stolen all his equipment and left him here in the jungle. It's not like it hadn't happened before. Once he got back to The Trust, Vincent would show them his harmonic knife and tell them he'd even found the lost city. He might even tell them about the terror birds.

He unslung the satchel, placed it on the floor, and pulled out his lifeline: a powerful short-wave radio. Vincent would be back at his main base within a couple of hours. He was already making a mental list on who he could use for the return trip.

As he adjusted the dial, his arm smacked against the black block, causing it to shift a fraction. Did he just imagine that? Vincent let go of the radio and placed both hands on top of the block and tried to push it. "Come on, you blasted thing," he muttered. It didn't matter what he tried, the black block refused to move. Vincent was almost ready to believe that his mind was playing tricks.

He sat cross-legged and reluctantly let go of the stone. He gently placed his elbow on the side of the stone, and pushed. The stone moved a couple of inches to the left. "That is incredible!" He pushed it again. This time, the block moved another inch before it sank into the smooth grey stone.

The floor shook. He jumped to his feet and tried to move off, but the stone suddenly dropped, taking him with it.

Vincent whimpered as the jungle floor receded. The grey stone square sank into the earth, taking him and his radio with it. His treasured satchel was still on the jungle floor. He must have inadvertently pushed it away when he was trying to move the stone block. Vincent felt like he'd just lost his best friend.

The grey stone came to a sudden stop. Vincent spun around and found himself looking at a huge arched entrance. He slowly got to his feet and approached it, his hands gliding across the stone. It was made from the same substance as the black monoliths. Vincent saw nothing but utter blackness beyond the archway. He shivered in fear and had to avert his gaze. Staring at that blackness made his eyes hurt.

It didn't matter that he had no other choice but to walk through that archway. Deep within Vincent's guts, he knew that only death awaited him in there. He hurried over to the smooth wall and looked up towards the surface. Vincent stretched his arms up, knowing it was a futile move. The only way he would be able to reach the edge was if he magically grew another ten feet.

The sound of something brushing past rock froze him solid. He was no longer alone in this chamber. Vincent flattened his palms against the hard dirt and tried not to scream when he felt hot breath close to his left ear. The shriek did burst from him when something covered the top of his head. He saw three fingers double the thickness of his own press over his forehead. The contents of his bladder released when the creature pulled him away from the wall and dragged him backwards towards the archway.

CHAPTER ONE

London 1988

Two sparrows fought over the remains of somebody's discarded sandwich. Dane Gerous smiled to himself when one of the birds pushed its tiny beak into the middle, pulled out a slice of white meat before flying off, leaving the remaining sparrow with two pieces of buttered bread.

He sat down in his usual spot and took out his own sandwich. "Don't look too upset about it, dude," he said to the sparrow. "You might have ended up with the crappy deal, but at least you're not going to be scoffing a bit from another birdy."

The mid-afternoon November sun took the edge off that bitter temperature that had already threatened to freeze the surface of the lake. Dane sensed this was going to be a bad winter. He smiled at an elderly couple, who replied with a couple of tuts as they walked past the park bench. Dane wasn't sure whether they objected to him chatting to the wildlife or that he was wearing a T-shirt in this weather. He watched the two of them head towards the bowling green, pausing to shout at a teenage boy skateboarding along the edge of the path.

That pair obviously needed a double dose of joy injecting into their sad lives. He tipped an imaginary hat when the skateboarder rode passed him before he began to fight with the cellophane wrapper wrapped around his lunch.

He had just over three hours before he was due back at the museum. Apparently, he was supposed to be giving a talk to a bunch of schoolkids about pre-Roman Britain. Dane hoped this crowd would be a little more receptive than the last lot from this morning.

Dane didn't so much mind the museum curator asking him to

do the occasional talk for the school parties. It kept old Harry happy, as well as giving Dane a steady income. It also allowed him to use all of the museum's extensive facilities for his own purposes. Unlike almost every other dome-brain who knew Dane, Harry hadn't even raised an eyebrow when he mentioned aliens.

A one-legged pigeon landed beside the sparrow, scooped up the bread, and flew off, leaving the little bird looking most upset. "Don't you worry, my friend. You can share this with me."

"Am I to address you as *Doctor Doolittle* now, or are we sticking to the traditional *Doctor Gerous*?"

Dane carefully peeled off the crust and threw it towards the sparrow, sighing when the bird took off without its prize. "How did you find me?" He didn't turn around. Instead, he took a small bite of the beef salad sandwich, while idly wondering if anybody would notice if he quietly murdered the middle-aged man now sitting next to him. He put the sandwich on the bench, not surprised to discover that he wasn't hungry anymore. Being in the presence of this odious individual did that to him.

"Do you seriously want me to answer that, Dane?"

He sat back and looked into the cloudless sky, still refusing to look at his face. "No, not really. Instead, why not answer this question? Do you want me to punch you so hard that you'll end up witnessing your own birth, or are you going to stand up, walk out of this park, and never come anywhere me again? It's your choice."

"Oh, so you're still a little upset. I thought you'd be over that by now, Dane."

Finally, Dane spun around and glared at the other man. Nelson Adams was three decades older than Dane. If the man was part of normal society, he would be looking forward to receiving his pension next year. Nelson Adams had never been part of normal society, and he certainly didn't need any pension money. Dane kept his hands by his side to avoid the temptation of punching this individual.

Until three years ago, Dane never considered himself to be part of normal society either. That all changed though, thanks to what this bastard did. "I can't believe you just said that, Nelson. No, wait. *Yes*, I can. After all, you sold your heart to Satan decades ago.

The only thing you have ever loved is money."

The older man leaned back against the seat. He placed his own hands, both wrapped in his usual fox fur gloves, on his lap, then slowly turned to gaze intensely at Dane. "I was there too, you know, or did that fact conveniently slip your mind? If it wasn't for me, it would have been you too falling down that shaft."

Dane closed his eyes and tried to force away the hurtful memories, but it did no good. Nelson's words triggered the avalanche.

He saw her terrified face, the girl who he'd sworn to keep safe, looking up at him, while she dangled over that stone shaft. His hands still slick with the hot blood belonging to the owner of this ancient building, but couldn't keep a tight grip on Lindsey May's skin. Dane remembered screaming for Nelson to help him. He remembered looking back and thinking the old man had run off, leaving him alone.

Dane turned back, only to witness the twenty-three-year-old woman's wrists slipping through his hands. He tried to hold on, to save her, but she just slid out. He vaguely remembered screaming while watching the woman fall to her death.

"Where were you, Nelson? Where were you when I needed you the most? Lindsey was our responsibility, and you let her die."

The older man's hand disappeared inside the pocket of his grey overcoat. "Is that what you think, Dane?"

The younger man stood. "It's what happened," he growled. "Look, it's been great, chewing over old times. It really has. Now though, I think you should go back to the rock you crawled from under." He picked up his sandwich, emptied the contents on the grass verge, and dropped the packet into the little bin before walking off.

This meant that he would have to disappear again. This time though, he'd have to make totally sure that The Trust wouldn't be able to find him so easily. Dane's father would be most annoyed at discovering that his only son had done a runner again, but he could live with that, even if Dad couldn't.

He turned around and saw that the bench was now empty. Good riddance to him as well. Talk about totally ruining his day. Dane paused when he spotted movement. A sparrow emerged from inside the litter bin with a strip of dark meat between its beak. "Well, it's good to see that your day isn't a total disaster, birdy."

The car was waiting directly in front of the park gate. As per usual, Dane ignored it and crossed over the road, intending to spend his remaining time in London browsing in one of the many shopping centres. A new toy store had opened west of Oxford Street. He could go there. It wouldn't only take him twenty minutes by tube. That sounded like an excellent plan.

He felt bad for having to let down old Harry and the school kids, but he had no other choice. It is highly likely that The Trust had found Dane through the museum. That organisation had contacts everywhere.

Dane strolled up the road and headed towards the nearest tube station, fully aware that the car was following him. He stopped, turned around, and glared as it pulled in and stopped. The window wound down.

"Are you sure you don't want me to drive you back to the museum, Dane?"

"No, thank you, Bradley. In fact, I don't want you or any more of Dad's stooges anywhere near me. Have you got that?"

"I can relay that message to Mr. Gerous. If that's what you want."

Dane nodded. "Yeah, I do want that. Now, why don't you go make yourself scarce, buddy?" Having said his piece, he turned and strode away, hoping the bodyguard that Dad had assigned to him would take the hint.

This was turning out to be a seriously crappy day. Dane blinked rapidly, feeling the tears already beginning to flow. God, after all this time, why did that bastard have to turn up and bring back all those terrible memories? He might have only known that poor woman for a couple of weeks, but Dane was beginning to fall in love with her. He stopped and gazed in a shop front window. He saw a man with a shock of unruly short blond hair lying on top of a thick set face, steel grey eyes, and a strong jaw line. He also saw a familiar car, parked up on the other side of the road. So much for the man leaving him alone.

Bradley was married; the guy had been with his wife for almost ten years now. They had two daughters and lived in one of the nicer houses on the outskirts of the city. Bradley was ex-army, ex-special forces.

Unlike Dane, he hadn't destroyed his life. That man had a future. What did he have left? His hand instinctively went to the necklace which Lindsey had given to him two days before she died.

The entrance to the tube station was just around the corner. Instead of carrying on, Dane doubled back and headed for a transport cafe that he passed a couple of minutes ago. The shopping trip could wait. Right now, he needed to eat. After all, it's what he had intended to do before the appearance of that bad penny ruined his appetite. He might even save Bradley a sausage. It must be hungry, boring, and lonely work having to watch Dane all the time. Still, Dane could at least provide Bradley with a little excitement by playing cat and mouse through the streets of London. There was no way that Dane would allow his father's main stooge see him leave the country.

He pushed open the cafe door, smiling as the smell of sizzling bacon caressed his nose. Dane took a seat in the corner, away for the window, and watched the waitress take the order from the only other man in the café.

This time tomorrow, he would be on the west coast of the US, probably tucking into a plate stacked with waffles and maple syrup. Dane would miss the good old British breakfast, but at least he wouldn't have eyes following him everywhere he went.

The waitress approached his table. Dane ordered a bacon sandwich, an extra sausage, and a large mug of tea. She smiled at him before vanishing into the back room behind the counter. Dane turned his thoughts back to getting away from here, trying to remember exactly how much money he had in the bank account that his dad didn't know about. Enough to buy a one-way plane ticket, certainly. There wouldn't be a lot left, though. Not enough to live on for more than a few weeks, meaning he'd have to find work.

That would be tricky. There wasn't a chance that Dane would be able to continue in his chosen career, not if he wanted to stay under The Trust's radar. He could always get a job in security. Just like Bradley, he'd been trained up courtesy of Her Majesty's armed forces. Wouldn't that be the ultimate irony if he ended up with a job which involved following people around?

The other man stood and walked towards the door. Dane silently groaned when he saw the grey overcoat and the fox fur gloves. Nelson pushed the bolt home, and spun the sign from *open* to *closed* before taking a seat opposite Dane.

"I'm not going to bother how you knew I would be in here."

The older man placed his hands on the table. He leaned forward. "Dane, I need you on this one."

"What part of *I don't want to see you again* did you not comprehend?"

"What part of *you don't have any other option* do you not understand?"

"Do you think that bolt is going to stop me from leaving, Nelson?" He leaned to one side. "I do believe that I can see my father's car right outside."

The other man sighed. "This isn't going how I planned."

"That's you all over, isn't it? I bet you didn't plan to run off, leaving me holding onto Lindsey either."

Nelson's eyes clouded over. He gazed down at the cracked pale blue Formica table. "I heard her scream as she fell, Dane. I also saw you running past me." The older man looked up. "I didn't leave you. No matter what else you think I might have done, I'm not a coward. I'd never run out on anyone."

"So where the fuck were you, Nelson?" he hissed. "I searched everywhere for you."

"The yeti that you shot fell on me. I had three hundred pounds of filthy white fur stuffed in my mouth. By the time I managed to get out from the under that corpse and get back to town, you had already gone."

"I don't believe you."

"That's your decision, Dane. I respect that. Believe me, I do. After all, you've allowed this to fester in your mind for three long years instead of facing it like a real man."

"Don't you dare try to psychoanalyse me, you *jumped-up nobody*. Not unless you want me to spread your nose across your face." Dane bit his bottom lip and attempted to calm down. The last thing he needed right now was to allow this man to wind him up. "So you think I'm eaten up with self-pity. Well, you're wrong."

"No, I don't think that. All I'm saying is that if you had come back to us instead of running away, we would have been able to resolve this. Look, what happened in Mongolia was an utter tragedy, but there was nothing we could have done to alter what happened."

Dane kept silent, still not trusting himself to reply. If what Nelson said was true, then he had wasted all those years blaming the old man for nothing. Finally, he leaned back and peered into the cafe back area, trying to see where that waitress had gone. She was taking way too long.

"If you are looking for the waitress, I gave her twenty pounds to make herself vanish. Don't worry. I don't intend to keep you long."

"What do you want, Nelson?"

"I want us to be friends, but as that's unlikely to happen anytime soon, let's just settle for you doing one last job for The Trust. For old times' sake."

"Why can't you get it into your thick head that I'm not interested in putting my neck on the line for the sake of some stupid artefact? I'm finished with The Trust. So please, leave me alone and let me eat my breakfast in peace."

Nelson shook his head. "Well, if your mind is made up, then I guess I might as well go." He rose and climbed out of the booth. "Oh, do you mind if I move this," he added, pointing to the metal salt cellar which stood with the rest of the condiments at the other side of the table. Without waiting for a reply, he leaned across and slid it into the middle of the table.

"What the hell are you doing?"

The older man smiled. "I'm leaving the cafe, just like you requested, Dane. Before I go, I just want you to witness what you are throwing away." He shrugged. "I so do enjoy rubbing it in, you know?"

Nelson reached into his inside pocket and pulled out something wrapped in dark green cloth. "This came into our possession not long ago." He placed it on the table beside the salt cellar and carefully pulled back the folds of the cloth.

Dane's eyes bulged at the sight of the exposed object. At first, he thought it was a ceremonial dagger, but the proportions were all wrong. Also, no self-respecting culture would use anything so plain. "Where did you find this piece?"

"Oh, so you are interested now?" Nelson shrugged again before he recovered the object. "Enjoy your breakfast, Dane." He picked up the piece and turned around. "I would say it's been a pleasure, but that would be a lie."

"Wait!" Dane jumped up. "Stop it with the bloody games, Nelson. Come back here, you bloody idiot."

The man chuckled. "Got you interested, have I?" He sat opposite and took out the piece again. He unwrapped it and placed the object on the table. "It's a blade. That much we do know." Nelson ran his forefinger along the thick handle. "We also suspect that no human created this." He wrapped his fingers around the handle. "Not unless they had very big hands."

Dane licked his lips. "Is it off-world?" He watched the other man turn the blade over and spin it until the hilt faced Dane. This could be the Holy Grail, the one piece that proved that Dane was correct about other civilizations visiting this planet sometime in its distant past. He looked into Nelson's eyes and wondered exactly what this man was playing at here. If this was the bait, then the older man had already caught him, hook, line, and sinker. "Well, is it not of terrestrial creation?"

Nelson laughed softly. "Now you're putting words into my mouth, Dane. I only said it was non-human. Nobody said anything about bloody aliens." He leaned over. "Do you still have the necklace that she gave you?"

"Wait, what's that got to do with anything?"

"May I see it, please?"

Dane sighed before pulling off and dropping the chain into his outstretched palm.

Nelson dropped the chain onto the table while keeping hold of the small green gem. "This is going to sound like a silly question, but have you had this gem analysed?"

"Of course I haven't! Lindsey told me she picked it up at Hackney market."

"And you believed her? You're more naïve than I first believed." Nelson dug his fingernail into the gap between the gem and one of the metal clasps, popping it out.

"Hey! I didn't say you could break it."

The older man picked up the diamond shaped gem between his thumb and forefinger. "What a remarkable piece of engineering. Totally flawless." He grinned at Dane. "Hidden in plain sight. That girl was more devious than we could ever know."

"Do you want me to stab you with this thing?"

"This is a green diamond, Dane. An artificially created stone." He pointed to the base of the hilt. "And we think they used them to power their devices." Nelson picked up the knife and pushed the gem into the slot at the base.

A low hum filled the area. Dane stared in astonishment as an apple-green haze now encircled the five-inch narrow blade. He'd never seen anything like this in his entire career, not even any hint that such a device had even existed. "What is it?"

Nelson placed the edge of the blade against the top of the salt cellar. He winked at Dane before sliding his hand to the left. The blade cut straight through the metal. Nelson pulled the gem out of the bottom of the knife, wrapped the object up in the cloth, and dropped it back into his inside pocket. He popped the gem into the clasp and handed the necklace back to Dane. "Are you still not interested?"

Dane dropped the necklace into his pocket, suddenly feeling very conspicuous about having it on display around his neck. He picked up the severed top and carefully pressed the tip of his forefinger against the edge and found it to be razor sharp. Dane's head was spinning over the implications of what he'd just been shown. He also couldn't discard the fact that Lindsey might not have been so much the innocent first-year research assistant that she had initially claimed to be. He placed both pieces of the salt cellar into his pocket.

"Where did it come from? What about the age? You must have a basic clue as to how old it must be? This is just unreal. The technology alone is beyond our present capabilities. Come on, Nelson. I know The Trust. They always know far more than they are willing to admit."

"That could really be true, my friend, but you don't want anything to do with us anymore. You said it yourself." The man looked into the back area of the cafe and gave a little wave. "You enjoy your breakfast, Dane. I'll be in touch, if you make the right decisions." He placed his hands on the edge of the table. "Take care of yourself."

"*Make the right decisions*, what the hell is that supposed to mean?

The older man strode over to the door and unbolted it. "You're supposed to be the archaeologist, meaning you're excellent at puzzles. Work it out." He left the cafe and disappeared around the corner before Dane could ask him any further questions.

The waitress gently placed a white plate containing his order on the table beside him. She then reached over and grabbed a salt cellar from the next table and placed it next to his plate. "Enjoy your breakfast."

CHAPTER TWO

The two suited men that Dane thought he had lost in the perfume section of that department store were now standing on the corner of Pickle Street, pretending to find interest in the window of a fishing tackle shop. Perhaps he ought to ask them if they wanted to swap windows, considering he was pretending to look into a shop that specialised in sex toys.

It couldn't be a coincidence that just three hours after meeting with Nelson, Dane would find himself being followed. They weren't part of his dad's security team. That much he did know. They were far too sloppy. He also discounted The Trust as well. Thanks to Nelson's theatrics, the bastards had already hooked him. They had no need to follow him around the city.

Whoever they were, he wasn't going to allow himself to be tailed. Dane waited for the traffic lights to change from red to green before he spun around and raced down the busy pavement. He took a left turn when he reached an alleyway. Heavy footsteps and annoyed shouting told Dane that his followers had managed to get over that busy road without being hit by a vehicle, and from the sound of it, they were catching up.

Dane stopped by a fire exit. He braced on the door, then vaulted over a high brick wall. A pile of black plastic bin bags broke his fall. He stayed where he lay for a moment and listened to two foreign voices shouting at each other. He grinned to himself, realising that the fire door belonged to the back of a Chinese supermarket.

He peered over the wall and listened as a middle-aged Chinese man told the suited gentleman to *bugger off* in Mandarin, while the suited gentleman replied in kind with a stream of insults in Ukrainian.

"I can see him!"

Oh crap. Dane hadn't noticed his other follower turning into the alley. The Chinese man slammed the fire door shut when both men produced handguns from inside their suit jackets.

He jumped off the bin bags and ran across the paved square, heading for the single door in the corner of the building. Dane pushed down the handle and pulled, and found it jammed shut. "I haven't really thought this through," he muttered, listening to their footsteps drawing closer.

A pair of hands appeared at the top of the wall, soon followed by a grinning face. It wasn't an expression of humour either. That was confirmed when the goon managed to get most of his body on the narrow top before aiming his handgun at Dane.

Dane ran back across the square, picked up the closest bag, and threw it at the goon. His aim was true. The bag smacked the suited man right in the face, causing the goon to let off another stream of obscenities in Ukrainian. He scooped up another bag and discovered a tiny pair of black eyes staring back at him.

He risked a quick glance over at the wall and saw the goon was trying to climb down. "Sorry about this, chap," he whispered, darting forward and snatching up the large brown rat. Dane whistled, and when the goon spun around, he flung the animal at the goon.

Once again, Dane's aim was true. The squeaking rodent hit the man's face, feet first.

The goon staggered back, dropped his gun into the rubbish, and cracked the back of his head against the wall.

"Let's go for the hat trick." Dane rabbit-punched the already-dazed man, then moved to the side as the goon fell into the bin bags. He retrieved the dropped gun then, pressed his body against the wall.

"Gregori, Gregori?" hissed a voice from the other side of the wall.

"He's down!" replied Dane, in passable Ukrainian.

Eight fingers and two thumbs appeared right above him. Dane waited until the man's head made an appearance before he jumped up, grabbed the back of the man's collar, and pulled him over. Dane followed him down and landed on the other suited man's chest. Before the second goon could react, he pushed the muzzle of the handgun against the snarling man's cheek.

"Why are you following me?"

The man's eyes rolled to the left.

Dane pressed harder. "What, you think I won't shoot you? Now come on, speak up or kiss goodbye to your face. It's an easy option."

The goon's eyes finally found his. "No, it is you who is to die here, Mr. Gerous. I hear my friends already."

Dane swore. He heard the approaching footsteps as well. "I should have stayed in bed." He flipped the gun around and slammed the metal handle against the man's temple. He grabbed the second gun and ran back over to the wall. There were another three already in the alley. He fired off one shot, finding satisfaction at the sight of them scattering like ninepins. Dane fired again when they got up a little too quickly.

Her ran back to the unconscious man, hurriedly removed his jacket and trousers, put them on, then dragged the man closer to the wall and covered him in bin bags. How long would it take the back-up goons to realise that he was no longer shooting at them? More to the point, how long were they willing to stick around? The local police were bound to be on their way here by now.

He picked up another bin bag and threw it over the wall. A couple of angry shouts told him the other goons were still there. Dane climbed onto to the wall and slowly maneuvered down on the other side. He stayed in the shadows, kept his face down, and limped slowly towards the light, ignoring their questions. Dane knew the bluff wasn't going to get him out of here. One of them was bound to spot the switch.

The sound of police sirens cut through the general hubbub. Here they came. His gunshots had brought London's finest to the scene. That was all well and good, but Dane had no intentions of letting the boys in blue keep him locked up while they sorted this out. No chance. He didn't appreciate complete strangers trying to kill him.

Dane turned around and fell to the floor. Two sets of footsteps approached his still body. He waited until the first one had reached him before Dane jumped up. He wrapped his arm around the goon's neck and pushed his stolen gun into his back. "We're going for a walk," he whispered.

He pushed the goon over to the fire door and banged on it one more time, hoping to God that the owner wouldn't ignore it this time. Those sirens were getting louder. He only had a few seconds left. One of the remaining goons raised his gun, only for another one to tell him to lower his arm.

One by one, the other goons turned and ran out of the alley, leaving Dane alone with his prize. "Just me and you left, laddie. Isn't that cosy?"

He grinned when he heard the door opening again. Dane pulled the goon through as soon as the door opened wide enough. It wasn't the Chinese man this time. Dane found himself facing a furious-looking woman armed with an evil-looking hatchet. She let off a stream of questions too fast for him to understand what she was saying. Dane got the gist of what she wanted, though. The woman wanted him and his friend out of her shop.

He shook his head, painfully aware that two police cars had just squealed close to the entrance to the alley. Dane reached into the goon's inside pocket. His fingers closed around the man's wallet. He pulled it out and offered it to the woman, while asking her to shut the door in Mandarin.

It didn't surprise him to find her attitude completely change at the sight of the bulging wallet. She pulled the fire door shut and laughed at the goon before leading the pair of them through the narrow corridor into the back of the shop. The woman stuck her head through the beaded curtains and asked for strong rope.

Dane pushed the goon down on a wooden chair. He stood back and smiled at the man. He guessed that his captured goon had only just cleared his teenage years, and unlike the seasoned player whose clothes Dane now wore, this guy was clearly scared.

"The woman wants to keep you." He stroked the barrel of the gun. "She just told me that your corpse will keep her shop in meat for the next two months."

"Please, I don't know anything," he said.

"Doesn't matter anymore." Dane stroked the man's cheek with the gun barrel. "I got everything I needed from the other two. Oh sure, they weren't going to talk, but the big guy soon changed his tune when I pushed my fingers into his pal's eyes socket." Dane leaned further forward, until his nose was almost touching the weeping boy's nose. "Unless you know anything different?"

The Chinese woman handed him some rope then told the young man that she was going to *cut his balls off*, in English. It took effort for Dane to keep a straight face.

"I only know that we were supposed to keep you in our sight. It's just that some of the boys thought that wasn't enough and—"

Dane jumped when the man suddenly fell off the chair and crashed onto the stone floor. Thick blood pooled around his forehead. He grabbed the old woman and pushed her to the side just as a vase beside the chair shattered. Somebody from outside was shooting at them with a silenced rifle!

"Are you all right?"

The woman nodded.

"I am really sorry about this," he said. "I didn't think there would be any danger to you."

"You call this danger? No, I call it fun." The woman patted the back of Dane's hand. "You go now. The police will be here soon. I'll stay out of sight until they do." She pointed to his gun. "Give me that."

"Are you sure you know how to use it?"

She laughed. "You think we reached your glorious country on a pleasure cruise?" She pulled the gun from him. "Not using, I sell, though." The woman pointed to a narrow grey painted door next to a window. "You go that way. It leads upstairs and onto the roof. There you go west. A hatch drops you into the meat market."

He kissed her on the forehead. "Thank you," he said.

She smiled back at him. "No problem. Most joy I've had in years."

Dane crawled over to the door she indicated, silently wished her luck, then threw himself through the door and ran up a flight of metal stairs while listening to the sounds of more police sirens, as well as the voices of a dozen officers, running into the supermarket.

He tipped his imaginary hat towards the Chinese couple before opening the door at the top of the stairs and thanked lady fate for providing him with such gracious hosts. Without their help, it's likely that whoever had tried to take him down would have succeeded. Dane stepped out into the sun and ran over to the only hatch he could see, hoping that this was the one that the woman had mentioned.

Not that he had any other choice. The police had called in a helicopter, and him darting across the roof was bound to attract their attention. He managed to push back the latch and slide the hatch back. He dropped down, seconds before the helicopter flew past the roof. They had probably spotted him, meaning the police would be converging on the market as well.

It did occur to Dane that perhaps losing Bradley an hour before he'd picked another tail wasn't one of his brighter ideas. It also occurred to him that old Harry was likely to be calling him all the names under the sun at about this time.

His first job, once he was sure of his anonymity, would be to apologise to the old fella for letting him down. He was intending to make his way up there anyway. After all, that's where the useless Bradley would be parked.

The hatch had brought him into a small grey room full of cleaning materials. Dane pulled off the jacket, unrolled the extra pair of trousers, and dropped them into a decrepit-looking janitor's trolley before he pushed open the door and lost himself in the sea of people outside the room.

As Dane shuffled along with the other shoppers, moving past the stalls, each one doing everything in their power to draw in potential customers, he seriously hoped that the Chinese lady was joking about cutting up that dead kid. He watched a butcher expertly jointing half a carcass for a moment before moving on, making his way towards the side exit that would take Dane out, opposite to where the boys in blue were gathered.

As perverse as it sounded, it wasn't only the Chinese lady who had enjoyed themselves at the sudden exposure to possible death. Dane found it hard to credit that he'd missed all this during his self-imposed three years of quiet solitude.

He took his thoughts back to the incident in the cafe, in particular to that look of *reserved triumph* which spread across Nelson's face when the gem from Dane's necklace snapped into the base of that artefact. Right now, Dane felt both excited and frustrated over his lack of knowledge over that thing. He needed more information, much more information. For a start, Dane would so love to know everything that Nelson knew. And, how the bastard knew that his necklace would activate the device.

Dane pushed through a crowd of old women, stood around a mother and her young child, each one making the standard cooing sounds. Over the chorus of their annoying noises, Dane overheard a more official voice emanating from the main entrance. The boys in blue were now inside the market and spreading out. This was his cue to get out of there. The determined way they moved suggested that they knew exactly who they were looking for. The side exit was a few more metres away by the side of a stall selling cooked meat.

He stopped in front of the glass counter and watched two policemen walk down the next aisle. They were stopping people at random and showing them a photograph. Dane's instinct for self-preservation kicked in when he saw a market trader point towards the door where he slipped into the market. It seemed like a ridiculous idea that London's police would be suddenly after him, but his instinct told him that it was the case, no matter how paranoid it was.

"If you come with me now, Dane, I should be able to get you out of here," whispered a familiar voice by his side.

He turned his head to find a man, who Dane believed dead, grinning up at him.

"I see from your expression that you're surprised I'm still alive?"

"Oscar Delano. I should have known that you would be involved with this mess. The smell should have given it away." The short, dark-haired man was another blast from Dane's past. Unlike Nelson, this vile rat would receive no redemption from him. "If we weren't in a public place, I'd smash your ugly face right into this counter." He moved, only for the man to grab his arm.

"Give me the harmonic blade, Dane, and I'll show you a way out of here. You do know that the filth are after you now?" The man shook his head and sighed loudly. "To think that you had it in you to murder those three men. They'll put you away for a long time for that, you know. Not even your millionaire dad will be able to save you from your fate."

Dane knocked the man's hand away. "Go stick it where the sun doesn't shine." He pushed his hand deep into his pocket and wrapped his fingers around the salt cellar, as Delano pulled out a short snub pistol.

"You really don't have a choice here. Hand it over right now, before the filth see you." He peered over Dane's shoulder. "They're almost on top of you, my friend!"

"Can I help you two gentlemen?"

Dane turned to find a young blonde woman smiling at him for behind the counter. Her lips melted to utter terror when her eyes noticed the gun in the other man's hand. Delano turned the gun to point at the girl.

"One word, pretty lady, and you die." The man turned his attention to Dane. "Let's try this again, shall we? No more delays. Give me the harmonic blade!"

Dane grinned at the man. "Found your father yet? I heard he left you for some dirty Thai ladyboy." The sounds of the approaching policemen were getting louder. Now, thanks to the addition of another gentleman, who'd just arrived on the scene, Dane felt a little more in control. "Oscar, why don't you look behind yourself?"

"Do you honestly think I'm so stupid?"

Dane watched with interest as Bradley efficiently pulled the weapon out of the man's grip before a highly focussed punch dropped Delano to the stone floor. "I'm so sorry about that, miss." He tipped his imaginary hat before following Bradley towards the side exit.

"How did you find me?"

"You never left my sight, Dane."

"Why the hell did you allow those monkeys to chase me all the way around London then?"

Bradley opened the door. He shrugged. "For fun?" The man hurried over to the maroon Range Rover parked illegally outside the market exit. He opened the rear door. "Best hurry, sir. Your dad and Nelson are waiting for you back at the house."

Dane walked up to Bradley, dug into his other pocket, pulled out a napkin, and unfolded it. "I saved you this," he said, grinning at the man's irritated expression. When Bradley didn't reach for the present, Dane pick up the cold sausage and bit it in half. "Suit yourself," he said, climbing into the four-wheel drive.

CHAPTER THREE

It didn't matter how much effort he put in his leg muscles, his feet refused to move. It felt like he was stuck in thick honey. Dane swivelled his head, noting that the swarm had reached the cave entrance. It had taken him a good minute to squeeze into this small chamber, and he considered that to be his greatest achievement today, considering Dane truly believed he was going to find his body stuck between the rocks.

Dane tried once more to move his legs and found he could shift them a few inches forward, as long as he didn't think about it. Instead of worrying about looking for somewhere to hide in here, Dane focussed on trying to stem the bleeding. One pointed shard of rock sliced through the side of his stomach as he finally fell into the chamber. The wound wasn't deep, but it had opened up a good few inches of flesh. Since the fall, he'd been pressing what remained of his blue shirt tightly against the wound. His efforts hadn't stopped his blood from streaming down his thigh and dripping onto the stone.

Strange how he felt no pain. Dane put that down to shock. The first of the swarm had reached the gap on the rock face. A wasp the size of a lion landed on the surface. Its front legs glided along the edge of the rock, stopping when it found the blood-stained shard.

Dane tore his gaze away from the monstrous creature and attempted to push his way further into the interior of the chamber. The little light available to him vanished as more wasps landed on the rock. He knew he'd made the worst mistake of his life when his feet crunched on something thin and brittle. Dane looked down and saw he was walking over a thick bed of bones.

In trying to get away from the swarm, Dane had taken refuge in their home. This is where the things had built their nest! The sound of their wings grew louder and louder, reaching ear-piercing proportions. He dropped into the ancient bones and clapped his hands over his ears in a futile attempt to block out the noise.

The wasps were all around his shivering frame. At first, Dane thought that the wasps weren't aware of him, that perhaps that somehow, their senses hadn't picked him up. That hope died when, from the back of the chamber, another wasp, twice as large as the others, crawled across rock and bone, heading straight for him. It was their queen.

The creature lifted its large frame and rose into the air. The other wasps moved out of its way. Dane knew that this was it, his life was to come to an end. If he didn't die from the shock when her fist-sized stinger pierced his tender flesh, then he would surely die when her baby hatched inside his paralysed body and ate its way out.

He pulled a huge femur from beside his hip and wrapped his fingers around the bone. The queen hovered directly above Dane, her dangling feet coming within inches of his outstretched arm. He violently thrust the bone up, aiming for the creature's head, only for the wasp to move out of his reach at the last moment.

Several other wasps had now landed around Dane and were slowly moving towards him. He scrambled to his feet and ran towards the arc of light, smacking any wasp which came within distance of his improvised weapon. He thanked the hundreds of deities he knew that the feeling of swimming through honey had finally left him.

The warm breeze coming from outside the chamber brushed across his cheeks. He was going to make it. The entrance was now almost in front of him. He spun around and found to his surprise that the wasps had not moved, they weren't in pursuit at all.

He saw no point in questioning his good fortune. Dane needed to get out of he before his luck turned sour again. He spun back around, grabbed the edge of the rock, and pushed his head through the opening and looked down.

Twenty feet below him, where the rock met the grasslands, over a dozen giant humanoids raced towards him. Each one carried a thick wooden stake, taller than Dane. He turned around and saw the wasps were now inches from his face. Dane screamed.

CHAPTER FOUR

"For crying out loud, man. Will you keep hold of his arms?

"I'm trying, Bradley."

Dane's eyes shot open. He saw his two friends struggling to keep him still. He managed to raise his head and found there was no sign of any wasps, giant or otherwise. Dane would have relaxed there and then put his experience down to a stupid dream, if it wasn't for the fact that he had no idea where he was. He blinked a couple of times and waited for his eyes to adjust to the dim light. One thing was sure, they weren't inside the plane anymore, nor were they on the surface. Dane had spent enough time underground to recognise the characteristics. He turned his head to the side, and his gaze rested upon a large collection of bones piled up against one of the walls.

"What the hell is going on?" He managed to sit up. Dane glanced over at Nelson. "What happened to us?"

Bradley got to his feet. He walked over to an upturned box. The man picked it up and walked back, placing it next to Dane's thigh. "Let's get you off the floor."

Both he and Nelson lifted Dane off the floor and gently sat him down on the box. He took a deep breath and asked the last question one more time while taking in his surroundings. This wasn't the chamber from his dream. Dane took some comfort in that. He wasn't sure how he would have coped with that scenario. He detested wasps.

"Tell me what you remember last."

He decided to keep the events of that dream to himself. "We all boarded the jet." Dane pulled up the bottom of his shirt and breathed a sigh of relief when he found the dream wound wasn't there. "Both you and Bradley were arguing over something, and then…" Dane frowned. "That's it, I'm afraid. Then I woke up here."

Bradley nodded to himself. "You fell asleep, Dane, missing the fun and games."

"We were shot down," continued Nelson. "The plane was about a hundred miles from the airport when…" The older man shivered. "Jesus, I've been in some scrapes in my time, but seeing that missile heading towards us through the plane window almost stopped my poor heart. In fact, I was kinda hoping that my heart did give out before the missile hit the plane. I did not want to be incinerated."

"Through luck, or design, it punched through the wing. I believe it was design." Bradley picked up one of the small bones scattered across the floor and casually used the splintered end to clean his fingernails. "There was no warhead attached. Whoever launched it obviously wanted us to live." He dropped the bone and rolled up the shirt sleeve on his left arm. "We hit the water pretty hard. I think the impact must have knocked me sideways, as that's as much as I remember." Bradley tapped his forearm a couple of times. "I did notice this a minute ago." He looked at Dane. "It's a puncture mark. I think we've all been drugged."

"Drugged?" He sighed to himself. That would probably explain the weird dream. His eyes had adjusted enough for him to discern more of their surroundings. He slowly scanned the inside of the large cavern, only stopping when he saw the three of them weren't alone.

There were another two individuals in the cavern. He squinted his eyes, trying to make out their features, a difficult task in this dim light. Dane looked up at Nelson. "We have company," he muttered.

"Yeah, I noticed."

"Who are they?"

Nelson shrugged. "Not sure yet. We haven't asked. We wanted to make sure you were okay before the introductions, you know?"

A young, dark-haired girl pressed herself against a smooth rock. Judging from her posture, she too had no idea what was happening. Her head shifted to the left. Dane guessed she had realised that she was being scrutinised. Her eyes found his. She released a quiet gasp before vanishing behind the rock.

"Your charm strikes again."

"Shut up, Nelson. The poor thing's probably scared out her mind." He stood, holding onto Bradley until he was confident that he wasn't going to fall over.

"Steady there, Dane," said Bradley. "Whatever they used on us was pretty powerful."

"You and Nelson check on the girl. See if you can find out anything." He let go of the bodyguard and slowly made his way across the cavern floor, heading towards what appeared to be a large bundle of rags.

The gender of the remaining individual became apparent when he groaned as Dane reached him. He dropped to his knees and gently turned over the body. "Bloody hell!" he exclaimed when he found himself staring into a face which he had not seen in over ten years.

The man on the floor opened his eyes. He saw Dane looked down at him and grinned. "Small world."

"Benedict Harris. What the hell are you doing here?"

"Synchronicity, old friend. I was about to ask you the same question. Don't just look at me with your mouth wide open. Stop looking like a dumb fish and help me up. My body doesn't appear to be functioning at full capacity."

"I believe that we have all been drugged."

"Oh, that probably explains why I feel like utter dog shit."

Dane helped the man sit up, watching him take in his surroundings. Finally, the man's gaze settled on the other three. Benedict smiled. "Looks like the band is back together. Isn't this jolly. I don't recognise the pretty lady though. Is she your new squeeze?"

Benedict Harris worked in the same field as Dane. Their paths had crossed on more than one occasion. The last time was almost five years ago, when the pair of them were both investigating the possible sighting of a tribe of halflings in Indonesia. "Why don't you tell me what you remember? As I'm sure that this isn't any of your doing."

"Oh, the faith you have in me really does warm my heart." Benedict got to his feet. "After all, it is you who have sold their soul to some shadowy organisation. Unlike me, who managed to stay freelance."

"Come on, Benedict, stop it with the guilt trip already."

"Fine," he huffed. Benedict frowned. "There's not much I can recall. I had managed to bluff myself into a group of researchers who had permission from the Mexican authorities to dig close to the Calakmul pyramid." The older man grinned. "Not that I much cared about their excitement. Although, I will say that two of those young researchers were rather pretty. Long straight blonde hair, Californian complexion, legs that went all the way up to their…"

"Yes, I get it. What were you there for?"

"Have you heard of the Calakmul dragons?" Benedict chuckled when Dane shook his head. "Didn't think you would. In the sixth century, Tikal ruled the region. The southern Mayan city was like a superpower."

"Yes, yes, I do know my pre-history, Benedict. What's your point?"

"I don't think that the Calakmul snake kings could have possibly sacked the southern cities without help, and that help was in the form of domesticated dragons."

"That's ridiculous."

"As ridiculous as your futile search of offworld intelligences? Look, it's irrelevant now anyway, considering our current predicament. As to your original question, Dane, I remember finding a hidden doorway and becoming tremendously excited, then in my last moment of awareness, I saw three men in ski masks coming at me." The older man got to his feet. He walked past Dane and tentatively placed the palm of his hand against the cavern wall. "That's interesting," he muttered. Benedict turned around. "When I awoke from a rather peculiar dream, I thought that those men had left me where I fell, but I now know that's not correct. Judging from the evidence, we are possibly a thousand miles south from where those thugs attacked me."

Dane didn't bother asking the old archaeologist how he could possibly know that. Instead, he turned and walked over to his two friends, hoping that they have had some luck in extracting some information from the girl.

The girl crouched beside the rock with her slender arms

wrapped around her knees. Unlike Benedict, she showed no sign of wishing to share her history. She didn't run back around the large rock when he approached her, so he took that as a positive sign. Although, her not moving could be down to his two friends standing at either side of her.

He crouched in front of her and slowly extended his arm. "Hello there," he said. "My name is Dane. It's okay, we're friends."

The girl didn't respond.

"I think she's in shock," said Nelson.

"My guess is that she just doesn't like you, Dane," suggested Benedict. "Or maybe your breath smells?"

"You're not helping here." Dane took off his jacket and gently placed it over her knees before standing. "Put that over your back, honey. It'll help take off the chill."

"We don't know where we are, who did this, or why. I'm taking consolation that we're not dead." Dane walked over to the only source of light, a circular hole the width of a small car, leading from the cavern ceiling to, he believed, the surface. There was no way that they were leaving through this route. Even if they somehow managed to find a way to reach the cavern ceiling, he saw no possible solution to scaling the inside of that tunnel. From what he could discern, the surface was as smooth as glass. The sunlight cast a perfect circle upon the cavern floor.

"Wait. Have I missed something here?" asked Bradley. "Just how is our continued existence a good thing?"

"Somebody has gone to some considerable trouble to bring us all together."

"I'm still not buying it, Dane." He glanced over at the girl before shaking his head. "It's more likely that we're to be held for ransom by a group of guerrillas, desperate for money."

"They can't that that poor," replied Nelson. "Not if they have the capability to take down our plane with a surface-to-air missile."

Dane looked over at Benedict. "If it had been anyone else other than him, I might have agreed. But don't you think it's just a little too coincidental to find ourselves with another scientist who is involved in our line of business?"

The older archaeologist chuckled to himself. He joined Dane directly under the hole. "I never knew you cared." Benedict tilted his head back and gazed towards the light source. "Still, it does seem rather over the top. I mean, if they wanted our help, couldn't they have just asked us?" The man's gaze then shifted. He took one step back and studied the cavern ceiling. "Shit."

Dane almost fell forward when the older man patted him hard on the back.

"I hope you're right, my friend," he whispered. "If not, then we really are in trouble."

He followed Benedict's gaze and noticed for the first time that something resembling wet cotton wool totally covered the cavern ceiling. "Is that what I think it is?"

"If you're thinking that the ceiling is covered in spider silk, then yes."

No matter how much Dane wanted to believe his own theory, Bradley's notion that they were walking bags of money for some half-crazed bunch of maniacs in camouflage refused to let go of his brain. "Pay now or they get eaten by spiders."

"Dane, are you okay?"

"Me? Sure, Nelson, never better. Come on, chaps, let's see if we can find a way out of this place."

"There is no way out," replied a loud voice from the shadows.

"Show yourself," growled Bradley.

"Over there!"

Dane followed Benedict's pointed finger and could just about make out another man at the far side of the cavern. He stepped out into the dim light, saw Dane, and scowled. Unlike the others, he carried a thick wooden pole, sharpened at both ends.

"You! This is all your fault, scientist." The man stopped a few feet from Dane. "I ought to stick you with this."

The archaeologist stood his ground. The man looked more frightened than angry. Even armed with the wooden stick, Dane was sure he'd be able to disarm him without causing the stranger too much harm. From the corner of his eye, he saw Bradley tensing. "Friend, I'm sorry that you're upset with me, but I'm sure we can resolve it. Look, why don't you drop the wooden pole, and then we can talk." He took one step forward, his eyes never leaving the stranger. "Perhaps we can all find a way out of here together?"

"There is no way out!" he hissed.

The man lunged at Dane. He neatly sidestepped the stranger, then brought his fist down on the back of his neck. Bradley had scooped up the weapon when the howling man crashed onto the floor. Dane dropped onto the man, pulled his arm around, and held them behind the man's back. "Now, let's start with why you appear to have a beef with me?"

"I ain't telling you nothing!"

"If you give me that pole," said Benedict, "I'm sure I could make him talk." The other archaeologist grinned at Dane. "I could have him singing like a bird in seconds."

Dane shuddered. "Nobody's torturing anyone." He slowly climbed off the man's back, then released his arms. "Perhaps we can now talk like civilised men?"

The stranger rolled over and hissed at Dane before scrambling onto his feet and running back into the shadows.

"Or perhaps not." Dane sighed to himself. Perhaps he should have allowed the older man to have a word with their new guest after all? He ran after the man, who had now taken up position against the damp wall. He pushed his fingers into the man's shoulder and spun him around.

"What?" spat the man.

His tone reminded Dane of some brash teenage boy, yet underneath all that bravado, he was clearly terrified. The fear didn't stem from Dane or any of the others within this cavern. Dane bit his bottom lip. He knew that if he wanted to learn the source, he needed to alter the man's priorities.

"You are going to tell me what I want to know, friend."

Judging from the sneer now plastered across the man's face, he failed to notice, or just ignored Dane's hidden threat. The man's look of sneer soon changed when Dane cupped the stranger's testicles. He slapped his other hand over the man's mouth, then gave the delicate balls a single vicious squeeze.

"It's nice to see your arrogance has vanished." Dane knew his words were wasted as his victim had something else to focus on; namely the wall of agony that had just slammed into his brain. He counted to five before removing his hand. The other hand stayed where it was.

"One more hint of insurrection out of you and I will squeeze again. This time, I won't stop until your bruised sac contains two crushed grapes. Do you understand me?"

"I was only supposed to undo the ropes and make sure you lot were safe." The man was now openly sobbing. "They said they'd come back for me once you had left. They promised!"

"Wait, slow down. Who did this?" Dane removed his other hand. All signs of resistance had totally vanished. "Please, start from the beginning, you're not making any sense."

He wiped his hand down his face. "What's to tell? They lowered you all down, one by one, through that big hole, starting with me. None of that matters though. Nothing matters. You see, there is no way out of here. I've walked around these walls over dozen times!" He slivered along the wall. "You're not going to hurt me again, are you?"

Dane shook his head. He already felt so guilty for being so savage in the first place. Despite the dire situation and this pathetic figure left him no other choice, Dane still felt like he'd just been caught kicking a puppy. "Please tell me who did this," he repeated. "Who's responsible for putting us down here?"

Instead of responding, the man slipped past Dane. He raced across the cavern floor, pausing once to scoop up the dropped staff. Dane resisted the urge to run after him. The archaeologist took his eyes off the shivering figure, he scanned the cavern, his gaze picking out each remaining face. They were all looking directly at him, including the girl. Just for that moment, he was tempted to see how she fit into this picture.

Practicality got the better of him. The reason didn't take priority. He allowed his gaze to dart towards the cavern ceiling. He shuddered. How long did they have before the inhabitants of those webs lowered their large hairy bodies towards their heads? They had to be nocturnal, meaning they didn't have long to figure out another route out of here.

"Benedict, got a moment?" The older man moved away from the young girl and made his way over. Dane wasn't keen on asking the creep for anything, but what other choice did he have? The man might have the morals of a donkey, but his brain was specifically wired for this kind of predicament. He just needed a suitable enticement.

"Did you get anything out of him?"

"Fragments, nothing concrete." Dane rubbed his stubbled chin, then leaned a little closer. "There's a door out of here, my friend." Dane looked past Benedict's shoulder.

"I almost turned him into a girl."

Benedict chuckled. "Yes, I heard. So much for not using torture." He smiled. "You're such a hypocrite. Okay, so a door. What else?"

"That's it, there's a door in here somewhere, and we need to find it as soon as possible."

"No, there's something else you're not telling me. Come on, spill it." Benedict's smile slowly faded only to be replaced by greed. "It's treasure, isn't it! Hidden gold." He nodded to himself and rushed over to the wall, muttering to himself.

Dane shook his head, then walked over to the others, vaguely wondering what drove a man to care more about material wealth than saving his own skin. Still, whatever worked. "Nelson, our friend was told that there is a way out of here that doesn't involve growing wings."

"Who told him?" asked Bradley.

"Our intimate conversation wasn't quite as detailed as I'd hoped."

"You should have hurt him again."

"Sorry, Bradley, I couldn't."

Nelson patted him on the shoulder. "You did the right thing," he said. "Even if it does end up getting us all killed." He looked up. "I saw you looking earlier. It doesn't take a genius to figure out what lives in here." Nelson took his leave and joined Benedict.

Bradley had already left him, preferring to comfort the girl than to keep Dane company. He walked over to the end of the cavern, trying to keep his temper under control. Would the pair of them had given him the hard time if he'd come down heavy on the girl instead? Like he needed an answer to that one.

"The next time you disturb me in the park, old friend," he muttered, "it'll be you who's going to be nursing a pair of sore testicles."

He flattened the palms of his hands against the rock and slowly felt his way along the surface, looking for any grooves or change in composition. Dane turned his head and saw Benedict and Nelson were doing the same.

"Do you think there is a door out of here?"

Dane tried not to jump; he hadn't realised that the bodyguard was standing behind him. He continued with his search, deciding not to answer the man.

"I mean, this is the sort of thing that you're good at, right?"

He turned around. "Are you doing this on purpose?"

Bradley grabbed the front of his shirt. "Thing is, Dane, for once, I agree with the old bastard. This really is your fault. I spent hours following you about. Have you any idea how tedious that is? Most of the time, though, you had no idea I was there. That's because I'm good at my job."

Dane felt something sharp pressed against his stomach.

"Yeah, that's right. I don't want to die down here, Dane, but, if that is the case, you won't be around to witness it."

"Move the knife, Bradley." When the bodyguard failed to comply, Dane took out his own knife and pressed the tip against the man's bladder. "I won't tell you twice."

Bradley grinned. "Mine's bigger."

Dane stepped back. He slipped his knife back into the sheath before pushing Bradley out of the way. He walked over to the hole and stood directly under it. He then got down on his knees and swept his hand through the sandy soil. It took him seconds to discover a flat surface beneath the dirt.

"What are you looking for?"

"There you go with the questions again, Bradley."

The bodyguard dropped to his knees, next to him. "Come on, what is it?"

"I'm looking for an arrow."

"You're shitting me. Like they are going to leave an arrow pointing to the way out."

"It's not a way out, it's a way in. We've just come through their front door, now we are in the hallway." He looked into Bradley's bemused face. "Living room, kitchen, reception room, secondary way out. They'll all be here."

"You don't know that."

Dane's fingers found the beginnings of a groove. "Yes, I do." He pushed away the remaining soil to reveal a line of seven circles, etched into the rock, pointing towards the rock face. The smallest circle, closest to him, was about the same size of a coin. The other six increased in size. Dane lowered his head and blew the sand out of the grooves.

"You are one big-headed bugger."

Bradley looked down at the pattern. "I'm not even going to ask how you knew." He pointed his arm parallel to the line of circles. "So, according to that, the door is right there." He ran over to the section of wall, stopped, and called Nelson over.

Dane watched the two older men hurry over to Bradley, while keeping an eye on the girl. It didn't escape his attention to find a slight smile had now appeared on her face. Before he could question her, she walked over to the other three.

He turned ninety degrees and began removing the loose soil again. It didn't surprise him to discover another line of geometric shapes pointing to the wall. Dane repeated the action twice before standing. He now had four lines of circles, squares, triangles, and ellipses. "One in four," he whispered. A shiver climbed up the base of his spine. Something told him that he was missing a vital part of the puzzle.

The strange man sat, cross-legged, watching the other four quietly. The staff lay across his thighs. Dane walked over to him. "Did you bring that with you?"

The man took his gaze away from the others and stared at Dane. "You promised you wouldn't hurt me again."

"I don't have time for this." He stooped down, snatched the pole, and walked over to the centre of the cavern. He heard the excited noises coming from Benedict. Dane guessed that he had found one of the doors. "One in four," he said again.

He held the pole by one of the pointed ends, then carefully raised the pole until the other end brushed against the ends of one of the webs.

"Stop it!" shouted the seated man. "Don't do that, don't wake them up!"

Dane ignored him and continued to push the tip of the pole into the thick silk. Something he dislodged tumbled out of the web. He dropped the pole in shock. Both the pole and the object hit the ground at the same time. "That's not good," he said, picking up half a jawbone. He twisted it around his fingers. It was human. Dane picked up the pole. Still, it did prove one thing: those webs were empty. It meant that they were either abandoned or the owners were out in the jungle, hunting.

"It's opening!" shouted Benedict. The man spun around. "Come on, don't just stand there!"

He watched all four of them take a single step back as a perfectly circular section of the wall recessed inwards before rolling to the side. Dane's heart skipped a beat when he saw movement within the dark interior. The bottom of his mouth dried up. The ceiling was alive with movement. None of the others had seen it yet!

"Get back over here," he shouted.

The girl shrieked as two spiders, each one the size of a dinner plate, crawled out of the opening and scurried up the wall. Bradley took her wrist and dragged her over to Dane, closely followed by Nelson and Benedict.

"Into the light! Get into the light." Dane pulled the two older men closer to him as the opening exploded with hundreds of long, black, fur-covered arachnid legs. "Get over here!" he yelled at the other man.

The remaining individual took no notice of Dane's frenzied shouts. He shrank back against the wall, shrieking as the horde of spiders ran over to the man and covered his body and head. Dane had to look away after he saw one of them had managed to crawl into the man's open mouth.

"And the Goddess, Ah Caax, takes her first sacrifice." The girl disentangled herself from the arms of Bradley. She hissed at Dane before running out of the circle of light.

Dane grabbed Bradley's arm to stop him from following her as she ran to the other side of the cavern.

She looked back once before placing both hands against the surface. In seconds, an elliptical part of the wall slid inwards and moved away.

"We need to go after her!"

Dane kept his grip on the bodyguard. "Don't be a fool! Christ knows what could be waiting for us in there."

The girl had already disappeared, and the wall had slid back into place.

"So, what, Dane?" spat Bradley. "We wait for those spiders to attack us next?"

He heard the man's accusation but refuse to rise. Dane was too busy searching through his memory to try to remember where he had heard the name *Ah Caax* before. The spiders had already started dissecting the poor man, starting with his fingers. Three of the arachnids were already crawling up the wall, each one holding a bloodied digit in their oversized fangs.

"Calm down," said Benedict. He pointed to the floor. "We still have another two doors to choose from." He grinned at Bradley. "Let's just all wish that the next door doesn't hold scorpions."

CHAPTER FIVE

Dane stopped walking for a moment to examine the markings on the wall by his left. He couldn't stop his mind from thinking that this was another dead end, another trap. The group had been walking through this narrow passage now for at least ten minutes, and apart from Bradley jumping at the sight of a single spider, their journey had been uneventful. Even Benedict had chosen not to speak. Even so, Dane still believed that opening up the triangle door was a bad idea.

What made it more maddening was going in this direction was his idea. Despite his prior warning, the others still wanted to follow the girl, their argument being that it was bound to be safe as she obviously knew this cavern's dark secrets.

"It doesn't fit with any Pre-Columbian script."

He turned his head to find the older archaeologist peering over his shoulder.

"Do you not find that a little strange, Dane?"

Benedict squeezed past him and walked a little further along the dark corridor.

"Where's he going?"

Dane shrugged. "No idea, Nelson."

The old man's torch light skipped from both walls until it settled upon the floor directly in front of him. "I think you might want to see this, chaps," said Benedict. "I think we might have a problem."

Dane rushed up to him, keeping his own torch light fixed on the floor. He skidded to a halt, just behind Benedict, his mind agog at the sight. There were four large eggs in front of Benedict, each one the size of a child's football. One of them had already hatched. He slowly lowered his knees. Dane extended his arm and shined the torch against the shell. "There's something in there, I can see it moving."

"They're too big for croc eggs," said Bradley "What are they, ostriches?"

Dane shook his head. "Wrong continent. Besides, an ostrich would likely split herself in two trying to lay these eggs."

"We need to go," murmured Nelson. "Like now." He started to back away. "Come on, we have to get out of here!"

Dane stood. He'd never seen the man looking more frightened. "What's wrong, man?" He gritted his teeth when he realised that, once again, Nelson hadn't given out all the information. He marched up to the scared man and gripped his shoulders. "What the hell have you gotten us into, Nelson?"

"I think I can hear something." Benedict walked a little further down the narrow corridor. "Yes," he announced. "We are definitely not alone in here. Perhaps it's the girl?"

"Amongst the other artefacts that ended up in our possession were a couple of claws and a single bone." He gazed into Dane's eyes. "They were from an animal recently dead."

"So what?" said Bradley. "What's the big deal?"

"What species were they from?" Dane's stomach had knotted up. He already guessed what the answer was going to be.

"They were from a terror bird, Bradley. A group of animals thought to be extinct for about a million years. The Trust could not find an exact match within the fossil record. The closest they found was a species called *Gastonis*, a nine-foot predator with a beak powerful enough to snap through a thick tree branch." The older man nodded over at Benedict. "Or cut through a man's thigh."

"Oh hell," he muttered, spinning around and running over to the older archaeologist. "Time to go." Dane grabbed the man's upper arm and dragged him back to the group. As he ran, the scratch of unseen feet running through the dirt reached his ears. All doubts that Nelson could have been mistaken about the egg's owner was extinguished when a terrible high-pitched shrieking echoed along the corridor.

"Back the way we came!"

"What the hell was that?"

Dane pointed at the eggs. "They are terror bird young."

Benedict skidded to a halt. "You're kidding! This is marvellous. Have you any idea how much they would be worth if we took one back with us?"

He couldn't believe the older man was serious, until Benedict pushed passed Dane. "Come back here, you fool!"

"I only need one egg."

The others were already out of sight, and as tempting as it was, he couldn't leave the older man behind, not after what had happened to the other man. Dane ran after him. "Have you lost your mind?"

"Not at all, young man." Benedict bent over and scooped up the smallest egg. He cradled it against his stomach. "Come on then, Dane. It's time to move."

"Not until you put that back. Not until you…" His remaining sentence dissolved at the sight of the single feathered monster slowly turning around the corner. Dane found himself trying to flatten his body against the side of the corridor in the vain hope that the creature wouldn't notice him.

From claw to head, the thing must have easily been ten feet high. Dane's scientific mind detached itself from his screaming subconscious and analysed the specimen.

He could understand why the white coats working in The Trust's labs believed they were looking at a Gastonis relative. The height was about right, so was the body thickness. The terror bird took one step forward. It lowered its neck and gently moved the remaining eggs around with its huge beak. Dane tried not to even breathe.

Gastonis has recently been re-classified as an herbivore, due to the shape of the beak. All bird species, extinct of otherwise, have hooked beaks. Gastonis didn't. This specimen's beak opened and closed, showing both Benedict and Dane the hook on the end of its beak. This thing was indeed a killer!

The older archaeologist backed away, stepping past Dane. He looked at the giant bird, then at the egg, still nestled against his stomach. "You're right," he hissed. "We need to move!" The man then turned around and raced away.

The terror bird let out a single screech of rage. Before it could move, Dane ran after Benedict, urging his legs to move faster than they've ever moved in his life. He heard the animal right behind him, and he knew that at any second now, he'd feel that wickedly sharp beak punch into the back of his head. He took no satisfaction in the fact that at least his death would be quick.

The older man was just in front of him. Dane now saw the others at the end of the corridor. Why had they stopped? Oh no, the door must have shut behind them. They were trapped!

Dane savagely pushed Benedict forward. The man slammed into the back of Bradley, dropping the egg. Dane dived forward and caught it before it could smash on the ground. He rolled onto his back then jumped onto his feet, holding the egg in the air. "Bradley, get that bloody door open!"

He watched the giant bird stop dead in its tracks. "Yeah, that's right, bitch. One more step and your precious baby becomes an omelette." If wasn't a Gastonis, then what the hell was it? Dane listened to Benedict mutter to himself as he tried to open the door. It did occur to Dane that it might not be possible to open the door from this direction, but he kept that information to himself. The giant bird lowered its head and squawked at him while ruffling its dark feathers. Its foul breath made Dane choke. That thing was certainly not an herbivore. He walked forward a couple of steps, watching the bird back off. "How are you doing with that door?"

"Almost there."

"Hurry up!" The terror bird suddenly turned its head to face the other direction. It let out another squawk; this time, it wasn't so loud. It then turned back to face Dane and cocked its head to one side. The bird then took one large stride towards him.

The egg in his hands no longer felt like the only thing stopping this huge animal from tearing Dane into flesh confetti. The bird lowered its head again and took one more step. It was just a couple of feet away from him now. Dane backed away, only stopping when his back smacked into someone else. "Hurry up with that bloody door!" he urged. The animal was about to pounce on them, he was sure of it.

"No way!" uttered a voice behind him. "Not another one!"

Dane then saw the unmistakable outline of one more terror bird quietly creeping along the corridor. This one was truly huge. It had to duck its menacing head in order to stop hitting the ceiling. It stopped by the clutch of eggs and released an ear-piercing squawk before it ran towards the other bird.

"I've got it. Come on!"

The smaller bird swivelled its head and let out a screech of its own before turning back around. Dane realised at the last minute that this animal wasn't the mother at all! He launched the egg at the bird before spinning around and following the others through the open triangular door. "Get it closed, Benedict! Hurry up."

The other man's fingers frantically danced across the stone surface, but no matter what he did, the door refused the close.

"We're going to die," said Nelson.

Dane backed away, keeping his gaze on the two huge birds, who were now almost at the doorway. "Come on, man. Get it closed!"

"It won't budge," he replied.

The two other men had retreated under the hole in the ceiling. The failing light made it difficult for Dane to make out the older archaeologist, Benedict. "Leave the door and get back here. Make sure you go around the cavern. Don't let the birds see you."

"I can't. I have to shut this door."

"Leave it. They won't come in here."

"How the bloody hell can you be sure of that?" demanded Bradley.

He kept his eyes on the birds while pointing at the ceiling. Already, he could hear the spiders getting reading to leave their webs. "Because those birds aren't as stupid as we are. I think the door will shut on its own accord."

Dane turned around, hoping that he was right about this. He ran over to the circle and pointed his torch before him. "There," he said. Dane shone the torch on the floor, illuminating the last markers before raising the beam of light until it reached the wall. "Go on, Benedict, repeat your magic."

The other man nodded then ran over to the wall, closely followed by Nelson. Bradley looked over at the two birds, still watching them.

"God, I wish they'd go away. Even better, the door shuts."

"Don't wish for that, Bradley."

"Why not?"

"Because, my guess is that once that door does shut, the spiders will drop. Come on." Dane ran over to the other two men, keeping his torch beam pointing to the floor. He wasn't sure how he'd react if he pointed it upwards just in time to see those eight-footed monsters descending.

While Benedict was getting to grips with the mechanism for the door, Dane took a moment to recover his breath and to attempt to control the adrenaline rushing through his body. It was also an effort to stop himself from grinning. Despite the horror of watching that poor man being killed by those spiders and knowing that the possibility of him meeting the same fate was very real, Dane couldn't stop the feeling of wanting more excitement.

"I think I can hear something," whispered Nelson.

"It's the spiders. I think they want their supper." Bradley grinned at Nelson. "If that noisy oaf doesn't hurry up with that door, the four of us will find ourselves in tiny little bits."

"Bradley," warned Dane. "Hush up."

Nelson pushed past him and pressed both his hands against the stone. "Hurry it up, Benedict. Get this damn thing open!"

The bodyguard stood right behind the man. "Listen, Nelson. Listen to them rubbing their hairy legs together."

"Enough, man!" Dane strode forward, ready to grab Bradley, just as the rectangular door slid open. Nelson fell through it, closely followed by the bodyguard.

Before Dane recovered, the door began to close. "Benedict, what the hell are you playing at?"

"It's none of my doing!" he shouted.

Dane grabbed the older man and dragged him towards the closing door. "Is there anything on the floor to stop it from shutting?" He reached the door and saw the narrowing gap, the other two watching helplessly on the other side. "Help us!" he shouted. "Find something to wedge it open."

Dane pushed his arm through the hole, only for the older archaeologist to pull him back. The pair of them fell to the floor. Dane watched both the doors, their only routes of escape slam shut, leaving the two men in darkness with only the sound of the thousands of waking spiders above their heads for company.

"What are we going to do now? We're trapped in here. None of the doors will open."

Dane got to his feet and pulled the other man over to the patterns in the floor. He used the torch light to find the remaining door, the one used by the girl. Dane then shined the light on the wall, moaning in horror at the sight of several large spiders crawling across the surface. He didn't need to point the light anywhere else to know that the rest of the walls would now be crawling with the oversized monsters.

He took off his jacket, turned it inside out, then ripped off one of the arms.

"What the hell are you doing?"

Dane passed the torch to Benedict. "Shine the light over there."

"Why? The door's on the opposite side."

"Just do it."

The other man sighed heavily.

He waited until the beam of light picking out the one item he needed before racing across the floor, avoiding three spiders falling from the ceiling. Dane snatched up the pole, wrapped the ripped material around one of the ends, then took out his lighter and set it alight. "Right, one last time," he hissed. Dane waved the blazing torch from side to side, thankful to see the spiders scuttle out of the light.

"What happens if this doesn't work? You said it yourself. These doors must shut when the light fails, to stop the spiders from infecting the rest of this place. Oh, you think this one is different, a master door."

"Will you just get that bloody door open? As for what happens if you don't? Well, I thought that would be obvious. We stay alive until we run out of clothing to burn." Dane glared at Benedict. "So unless you want to die screaming while those hairy bastards crawl over your naked body, I suggest you stop talking and do as you're told."

CHAPTER SIX

As per usual, the stupid bitch spilled most of his grape juice down her flimsy top. Instead of berating her, as his standard mode of approach to the idiot, Marlon gave her a lazy smile, then tapped the pine table three times with his index finger, then once with his forefinger.

She mumbled a grovelling apology before backing away.

"I don't want to hear those pathetic words ever again. Do you understand?"

The Dionysian slave nodded solemnly. Marlon repeated the motion with his fingers upon the table once more. "That will be the second to last time you see me do that. That next time I do it, I will scoop out one of your eyeballs, then push my arm through the hole, and squeeze your stupid brain in my fingers." He straightened his back. "Now, stop nodding your head and get me another drink."

Marlon waited until the slave had left his control room. He turned around and saw the girl he'd left with the captured group glaring at him. Normally, Marlon would have had anybody daring to look at him in that disrespectful way whipped. After what he had just witnessed via the camera, his mood was considerably better than most days, so he left the glower slip. "What's the matter, Itzel? You look," he paused and slowly licked his lips, "you look a little upset, my dear." He pushed back his high-backed chair and stood. "Are you put out because she gets more attention than you?"

Two of his fellow staff sniggered.

"One of these days, that woman is going to snap. I so want to be there when that happens, you evil little man. She'll tear off your arms before you can blink."

Marlon gave her an impatient flick of his hand. "I'm sure that would be totally possible, in an alternate universe." He gave her a withering smile. "But not this one. Now, if you've finished being annoying, perhaps you could make yourself useful and bugger off?"

"Wait, what about our agreement?"

"What about it? The goods I desire are still not in my grasp, young lady. Until that happens, your children stay where they are."

Marlon enjoyed watching the cauldron of volatile emotions swirling around her face. He almost made a wager with himself to see which one came out on top. He wanted her to say something very naughty, something that would guarantee her demise, closely followed by her two little brats. Instead, she sighed to herself before spinning around and storming out of the room. He gave her a little wave before sitting back down upon his chair in order to survey his new kingdom.

His stupid slave reappeared with another drink. Marlon waited patiently for her to finish, resisting the urge to flick her ear, just to see how she'd react. She finished pouring the drink and retreated to safe distance, keeping her head bowed at all times.

"Thank you," he said. "Now that wasn't too difficult. You may go."

He watched the giant slave take her pathetic form out of the room before re-positioning himself back on his chair. The sounds of keyboard tapping, coupled with the occasional cough, reached his ears. Now that the focus of his annoyance and amusement had left, the remaining four males in there with him would not dare to look away from their monitors for fear of him lashing out.

Marlon sighed to himself before turning around to continue his observation of his guests. It pained him to admit that he would miss the verbal battling, which he performed on a daily basis with Itzel. Despite the hold he had on her, she had never been shy to speak what was on her mind. It didn't seem to matter to her that her outburst was likely to cause him to reply in kind.

His staff were all too aware that he wasn't exactly the most stable of employer. Marlon flicked a couple of switches on the control panel which activated the cameras within the area, which the two archaeologists had found themselves in. As the area wasn't lit, he had to alter the spectrum to *infrared* in order to make out their forms.

As he followed their progress, Marlon recalled Itzel's warning regarding the slave. She was spot on about the giant. Standing at just under ten feet and weighing at almost six hundred pounds, she certainly was capable of killing any one of them without breaking into a sweat. He operated the joystick and moved the camera forward, smiling slightly as Dane wrapped one of his remaining scraps of jacket material around the charred pole and lit it. Marlon quickly switched to normal vision.

He watched the pair of them stop to examine a collection of geometric shapes etched into the wall beside Benedict. Judging from their facial expressions, they were having some kind of heated debate. He so wished he could hear their voices. Marlon would have killed to hear their conversations.

Still, the audio didn't really matter, as long as his maze rats led him to his goal of finding more giants like the idiot child presently in his service. Marlon leaned back and closed his eyes, allowing his fantasy of a huge army of captured giants rampaging across the land. Marlon chuckled to himself. To think that his father always believed that Marlon Dale would never amount to anything. Well, he'd already showed that loser who was the winner in this game.

"Sir, I think we've found the others."

He snapped open his eyes and turned his head. Young Adam Lumley stood in front of Marlon's desk, his head bowed and his posture submissive. His large brown eyes blinked once. God, what a sad individual. He was desperately waiting for his master to say that he was a good boy and give him a treat.

"Good man. Patch their location onto the main screen. Let's see where they are." In moments, he discovered that the sidekicks were doing significantly better than their masters. He watched, his jaw wide open as the pair of them wandered around several black monoliths. Each stone towered over the two men. The bodyguard ran his hands over the smooth stone. Marlon leaned a little closer to the wall-screen, secretly hoping that his interaction with the stone would somehow activate some kind of defence mechanism which would severely incapacitate the big-headed fool. Marlon found himself instantly hating that man from the moment he set eyes on him.

Marlon was so annoyed to find his hope of a mutilation didn't arise. "You're too lucky for your own good, you are," he muttered. "That's close to the south exit, isn't it?"

"Yes, sir," replied Adam. "They won't be able to go much further. That path stops at a stone wall. They'll have to turn back."

He found himself nodding at the eager puppy's statement. His interest with the sidekicks had already waned. He told the puppy to switch screen locations. He saw the archaeologists running their fingers across black stone. Unlike the dim-witted clowns, at least they looked as though they were slowly beginning to make sense of the patterns upon the walls.

Marlon pushed his keyboard to the left and ran his own fingers along the stone surface. There were no symbols below his equipment but, he knew from painful experience, that the absence of ancient writing did not mean that there was any hidden opening. This room was secure though. That much, he was sure about.

He nudged the keyboard back into place while watching the two archaeologists converse. Once again, he wished he could hear their words.

The cameras, like the rest of the equipment, initially belonged to his father. Marlon cast his gaze around the small room. In fact, everything in here belonged to the old man, including those four technicians, all doing their best not to return his stare.

James McBride was one of the wealthiest men on the planet. Not that the public knew of this. The man guarded his anonymity. Needless to say, though, the ordinary Joe on the street would have no doubt used something in his day-to-day existence which belonged to Marlon's father. He owned everything from electronics companies to national airlines.

His father would have no doubt disapproved of Marlon's little side-line if he knew of it. "That's one talent we do share, Daddy," he whispered. It appeared that although he had gained his slender physical traits from his mother, as well as her brown hair, brown eyes, and quick temper, Marlon had, at least, acquired his duplicitous nature from the old man. He pondered on this for a moment. Perhaps, if he felt really generous, Marlon could say that his almost fanatical pursuit of his life goals had come from him as well.

Marlon had no desire to become this world's invisible uncrowned king, to be the man who owned everything and everyone. He just desired to watch the world around him burn without getting scorched. It was perhaps a rather grandiose vision, a notion which should belong to madmen and egomaniacs.

He cast his thoughts back to that dark time in his life, when deep inside, Marlon felt he was lying on a broken raft, cast in the endless ocean of life. His inner-self couldn't decide whether he was about to sink and drown or to keep hanging onto what remained of his raft while the ocean currents took him around in a huge circle.

Looking back, perhaps it was the endless supply of half-naked beautiful women, drugs, booze, and tropical sun which provided the catalyst for his future ambitions. His father didn't want anything to do with Marlon. In fact, Marlon seriously believed that the old man privately hoped that he'd end up overdosing or drown in one of the family's many swimming pools. Marlon was one of his father's few mistakes, a genetic throwback, a fault to be swept under the carpet.

It occurred to Marlon that he could hear the sound of his breathing. The room had gone deadly quiet. Even the guys typing away were doing their hardest not to make a sound. He knew why, obviously. The four of them were on tenterhooks, waiting for him to detonate. Well, that wasn't going to happen. Despite the few snags, Marlon believed that everything was going to plan. His volatile temper would stay locked up in that box.

Strange that the older he became, the easier he found it to control the anger. That thought made him smile, considering he now realised that the old man must have hoped that Marlon's inability to control his volatile emotions would have caused Marlon to self-destruction all those years ago, back when he was a teen.

Would his dad have opted for Marlon to going down the road that should have ended in his demise if Marlon was an only child? Like he really needed an answer to that question. Of course he would. The old man had done everything in his power to stop Marlon from inheriting the family fortune.

Marlon didn't blame him. That, he guessed, would have shocked his dad *rigid*, but it was true. Marlon was a mess. Even if he had been groomed for the life role of CEO, Marlon still would have ended up destroying his dad's hard work in a matter of months. Not because he was incompetent, but because he wanted to.

His elder brother, Brian, fitted all the requisites needed to take over the family empire. Private schooling, followed by the best university in the country, as well as first class training from his father. Again, Marlon held no malice against his brother. As far as he was concerned, Brian was welcome to the business as long as he left Marlon free to pursue his own agenda.

He watched Adam's face turn as white as a sheet. Marlon then realised that he had been smiling at the young lad. "Do you not have something to do, Adam?"

The boy swallowed hard before returning to his duties. Perhaps he should remember to control his facial expressions in the future. Marlon had the idiotic grin plastered over his face because, thanks to him thinking about his dozy brother, an unwanted memory segment had just popped into his head.

Back before Marlon's hormones had turned him into every nanny's ultimate nightmare, Marlon had the run of the house. He could go wherever he desired, as long as he kept himself invisible and didn't enter the restricted areas in the house.

As Marlon wasn't allowed to leave the house, he spent most of his time in the library, losing himself within the pages of the many classics stored upon the shelves. The library was also where his dad used to tutor Brian. As long as he stayed silent, his dad didn't mind Marlon staying.

He didn't really pay much attention to the man's droning sentences. The characters within the stories generally demanded his full attention. There was one occasion, though, when his father's lessons did worm their way into his head.

His father was saying that their life was segmented and each section was defined by one major occurrence. The trick was to foresee the occurrence and choose the correct path, as travelling down the wrong path would inevitably lead to destruction.

The words might have been meant for Brian, but it didn't stop that from resurfacing seven years later in Marlon's drug-addled head.

He had woken up in the library of one of his father's associates. Lifting his head, Marlon saw the floor covered in bodies, arms, and legs sprawled over each other. As per the course, Marlon had no details of the events from the previous night. Although judging from the fact that most of the other people were naked, a large amount of sex might have been involved.

That didn't come as a surprise to Marlon. It seemed that every night terminated in the same fashion. He sat up and looked across the flesh carpet. He had no idea who any of them were. Again, this wasn't unusual. Procedure dictated that he should find a table occupied by scotch and the white stuff, and use enough until either he could no longer see or he came around enough to put some proper food in his guts. Today, his apathy towards his Groundhog Day situation was around to help him find that table.

As he untangled his limbs, got to his feet, and wandered around the library, Marlon decided that his apathy was probably still sleeping, no doubt under one of these perfectly proportioned female bodies. As he made his way towards one of the wall bookcases, attempting to avoid fingers, ankles, and hair, Marlon's head kept repeating the words his father once said to his brother regarding how life is segmented.

By the time Marlon reached the bookcase, those words had become a mantra. While those words were spinning around his mind, Marlon's thin forefinger slid along the book spines. Unlike the library where those words were one uttered, he saw no works of fiction anywhere. The shelves were packed with volumes of everything from ancient history to philosophy.

Marlon picked a book at random and tiptoed through the bodies while holding his prize tightly against his chest. He pushed the bottles and a saucer full of cigarette stubs, beer, and coke onto the floor, opened the book, and settled down to read.

After several hours of filling his head with several volumes of archaeology, ancient history, and prehistory, Marlon finally looked up from the pages. He was alone, cold, and very thirsty. Despite the discomfort, he couldn't stop smiling. His mind, starved of knowledge for several years, had soaked up the information like a dry sponge. He also discovered that his father's mantra had vanished.

Two days later, Marlon stood in front of his father's desk, dressed in the best threads money can buy, listening to the old man conduct half a dozen conversations on phones and with his minions who kept running in and out of his office.

When the old man finally found time to listen to his youngest son, Marlon repeated the words he once said to Brian. The flicker of surprise cast on his father's face, before the usual expression of disgust and annoyance only reserved for Marlon, settled in. The old man's return to form didn't bother Marlon one bit. Why should it? After all, for the first time in his life, he had a purpose, a quest.

Whilst reading and absorbing all that accumulated knowledge, Marlon became aware that hidden inside certain texts lay a code. A hidden pattern of clues and hints which, once solved, could unlock the way towards the greatest discoveries ever found.

Marlon told his father that he had found his purpose in life and needed equipment, staff, and funds. As predicted, the bastard burst out laughing. That hurtful sound soon stopped when Marlon explained that it was only a matter of diverting the money his father had put aside in order for Marlon to drink himself to death with. Of course, his father demanded to know exactly what exciting new venture he wished to waste his life on. Marlon simply replied with one word.

With a secret smile, Marlon said, *Antiquities.*

Marlon pulled his mind back to the present day. He had achieved so much since walking out of his father's office. He had secured funding to last him a lifetime, enough equipment to fill several office blocks, and a steady supply of his own closed-mouthed minions.

To use one of his father's favourite quotes, he needed to stay focused on the task at hand. Marlon might have come a long way in twenty years, but if he didn't concentrate on the moment, he could end up losing everything.

"Sir, I think we have a problem."

Marlon spun around. "What problem?"

"The two archaeologists," replied Adam, nervously licking his lips. "They have just vanished."

"How can that be? That's just a corridor, leading to one of the outer chambers." Marlon's fingers danced across the console as he rewound the surveillance tape. They had indeed found another doorway, one which his team had missed. This was excellent news. He paused. Also bad, as he could no longer keep a track on them.

Marlon re-watched the video feed as the pair of them studied the geometric symbols engraved in the stone wall. They were identical to the symbols on the floor in the previous room. Marlon then growled to himself and thought back to when the girl ran out of that chamber. "I can't believe I missed that!"

Marlon snapped his fingers. "Somebody bring the strong-willed native back to me. I want to have a word with her."

He watched the two men walk through the doorway and out of his field of vision. He couldn't believe it. The men had actually found another exit. One that his team had missed. Marlon slowly turned around when he heard footsteps echoing along the stone floor.

The native girl stopped a few feet from him and gazed defiantly at his face. She was a proud one, make no mistake; as slippery as an eel and about as trustworthy as a rat. She was also very beautiful. The girl knew it too, and she tried to use her looks on his staff at every opportunity. He knew for a fact that a couple of the weak-minded fools had given her a few treats in exchange for some special favours. Marlon had cameras installed in areas of this ancient city where even his staff didn't know.

Would she place those slender hands on her hips and pout, waiting for him to tell her what he wanted now? Marlon smiled to himself. Oh yes, there it was. She might possess the qualities which enabled her to survive in his presence without turning into an arse-licking worm-like the rest of them, but Itzel was also predictable.

"Itzel. I have always been honest with you, and I expected you to return the favour. So, why did you not tell me that you understood the ancients' language?" Her posture took a turn for the worse. She no longer looked like the universe owed her a living. "Are you going to deny it?"

The girl simply stood still, refusing to speak.

"Fine, that's perfectly fine. You keep quiet. I'm happy with that." Marlon stood and turned to Adam. "It's time, young man. A little sooner than I expected but," he glared at Itzel, "but, no matter. We shall overcome every obstacle."

Marlon clicked his fingers. When his slave came lumbering out from her room, he gestured her over. "Time to get your boots on, we're going for a little walk."

CHAPTER SEVEN

There was something to be said for possessing a thick, sharpened stick. For a start, the makeshift weapon had finally wiped that scowl from Bradley's face. Its usefulness against one of those giant birds remained to be seen. Nelson shivered to himself; he'd rather not be placed in that situation. Bradley's teddy bear replacement might fare better than a fist against a frenzied attack. Still, it wasn't quite an automatic weapon. There was no loss if the stick made the thug happy.

Happiness. Now that was a currently alien notion. It took some back-pedalling to recall the last moment when that emotion graced itself with its presence. In fact, the last occurrence would have been the moment when The Trust gave him this assignment. He knew there and then that he just had to involve his old friend, Dane, in this adventure.

He leaned against the cold stone wall, watching his companion whittle a cluster of six-inch grooves into the thick wooden shaft. Nelson's plan hadn't exactly gone as he'd expected, which was a bit of a surprise considering the amount of work Nelson had put into the initial preparation. Unlike Dane, and the bodyguard, he knew exactly what obstacles and dangers his team would have to overcome.

Nelson didn't foresee that crazy Marlon would try to blast the plane out of the sky, nor did he expect that freak to bring in another archaeologist. He used that title in the broadest possible terms. Grouping that charlatan into that revered category was like saying Bradley could read without opening his mouth. Still, it could have worked out a lot worse than it did. That megalomaniac's missile could have hit the fuselage.

He patted his pockets yet again and ground his teeth in frustration. How was he expected to survive this journey without his tobacco and pipe? The only items left in Nelson's pockets were a plastic bag containing some waterlogged fluff, five unidentified silver coins, and a note with a set of coordinates written on one side. None of the items belonged to him. Right now, he couldn't give a monkey's ass what game Marlon was playing. All he wanted was a bloody smoke.

"Are you okay?"

"Sure, just a little tired. Nothing to worry about." Nelson lifted his head and attempted to give his colleague a reassuring smile. After all, practicality demanded that he kept the thug appeased and calm. Considering the dangers that would be facing down here, Bradley needed to stay focused on the job of keeping Nelson alive.

The bodyguard shrugged. "Fair enough." He then went back to finishing off carving his stick. "Are you going to find us a way out of here?"

So much for the thug showing empathy. Nelson thrust his hands into his overcoat pocket and strode past Bradley, heading for the largest monolith in the chamber. He stopped in front of the giant black stone and gazed up, trying to see any imperfections on the smooth surface. It was a miracle of engineering, that's for sure. Then again, he already expected to find that even before they set off. The device that he showed to Dane already proved that the original inhabitants were centuries more advanced than their human relatives.

If he had that device, they'd be able to cut a way out of here. Nelson ran the coins through his fingers while considering their options. There was no obvious way out of this chamber, but that didn't automatically mean one didn't exist. He cast his gaze onto the dust-covered floor. Their footprints revealed stone paving. He saw nothing which indicated that others had been trapped in this chamber, yet he did notice evidence that they weren't the first humans to step foot in here. Bradley's stick was a prime example. Like that pole, grasped by that now dismembered chap from the other chamber, the one in the thug's hand possessed a sharp point.

Nelson saw no bones either. He walked over to the only object that looked like it didn't belong. "That's strange."

"What's strange?"

Nelson bent down and scooped up the object. He had just found a silver watch. Judging from the weight and the intricate workmanship, this piece was worth a pretty penny. It wasn't that old either. Nelson held it by the metal strap and showed it to Bradley.

"The second arm is going around!" Bradley snatched the watch from Nelson and held it close to his ear. "It's ticking, too. Do you know what that means?" Bradley dropped the watch into Nelson's open palm. "It means that somebody has been here recently."

There were no flies on this one. Nelson bit back a retort and simply nodded. He looked back at the floor. Now that he knew what he was looking for, Nelson could make out another set of footprints disturbing the thick dust. They didn't continue towards the wall, they turned around and headed back to the entrance where they'd fallen through. There was no point in rechecking that exit. Nelson had already figured out that when they had hit the floor, a deadbolt must have triggered.

"This means there's bound to be another way out of here, Nelson." Bradley ran over to the wall and started to run his fingers along the stone. "Shouldn't be that hard to find."

The poor deluded fool. Bradley obviously didn't see that the only footprints near the wall were his. Nelson now understood why he'd chosen the career of a bruiser. He'd be useless as a college tutor, unless his students needed their heads kicking in.

Nelson lowered himself to the floor and rested the back of his head against the wall. Was he being rather harsh with Bradley? Probably. He knew from previous experience that the chap wasn't a complete meathead. It might be childish and immature, but it certainly made Nelson feel better.

Once again, Marlon found his fingers drifting into his pocket and reaching for those five coins. Of everything that had happened to him and the others ever since waking up down here, it was the appearance of those silver coins which plagued him more than anything. Nelson knew there had to be some valid reason, some meaning behind them. The annoying thing about it all was that if he'd showed them to Dane as soon as he'd found them in there, the chap would have solved the puzzle in ten seconds flat.

Of course, that meant having to explain everything to him and the others. Nelson glanced over at the thug. Right now, he was trying to scoop out a line of dirt with his pointy stick. From his actions, it looked like the idiot had finally realised that the white rabbit hole wasn't going to magically appear after all.

Bradley would murder him if he ever discovered just how deep his involvement went with the organisation who orchestrated this whole mess. He wouldn't understand any of it, but that wouldn't matter. As far as Bradley was concerned, Nelson was the betrayer, the turncoat, the one who deceived his friends.

"Oh shit," he gasped. "No way, it can't mean that!" Nelson slammed a hand across his mouth. Had the thug heard him? He counted to five while watching him push his stick further into the hole he was making. Bradley looked like a dog burying a bone. No, he was too engrossed with his own thing to notice poor Nelson finally solving the problem.

Is that what Marlon was trying to say to him, that he was another Judas? Five wasn't exactly thirty. Then again, he wouldn't be able to lift his coat off the floor with so much metal inside his pocket.

There had to be another explanation, there just had to be. That fat, boss-eyed psycho didn't strike Nelson as a man who went for leaving cryptic clues. He'd never been that great at being subtle. Him blundering about was the whole reason as to how he'd ended up as a very loud ping on The Trust's radar.

Until the sudden appearance of Marlon, The Trust believed they knew of every unconventional adventurer and archaeologist in pursuit of the strange, weird, mythical, and downright ridiculous. It was, of course, utterly impossible to try and keep track of every crackpot who believed in Bigfoot or that the government was covering the existence of aliens, or that the biblical Nephilim giants still walked amongst us. Nelson's superiors believed that Marlon belonged to the latter category. Or, perhaps, because of the seemingly unlimited amount of funds available to him, Marlon should belong to a category made just for him—a billionaire nutter.

The Trust only became more interested in this strange little man when an article appeared in a South American newspaper, claiming that some European had not only found proof of the existence of the Nephilim, but had even captured one.

The interest changed to *involvement* when an agent for the Trust returned with photographic evidence, as well as information regarding news about a Trust-funded expedition from 1968. Once that was mentioned, then Marlon became a Trust priority.

"I think I've found something."

Nelson got onto his feet and attempted to look excited. It was unlikely that the thug had found anything other than a few bugs and more dirt. The man didn't turn around, he just continued to push the now blunt point into the widened groove. Bradley had succeeded in isolating a small stone by scooping out most of the dry mortar between the stones.

"Even if you remove that stone, we're not going to fit through the tiny hole."

Bradley stopped his exertions and turned his head. "Are you taking the piss? I'm not an idiot. I think there's somebody behind here. Can't you hear the noise?"

He could hear something, now that Bradley had moved the stick from the wall. Nelson placed his ear against the stone. It sounded like there was another Bradley on the other side of the wall armed with a pointy stick.

"Move out of the way."

Nelson threw himself to the left when he saw the look in Bradley's eyes. The man looked manic. He ducked past the man and tried to regain his composure while the weirdo started to punch the wall.

"You're going to break every bone in your hand, you bloody idiot!"

The bodyguard stopped. He turned around and grinned at Nelson while showing him his fist. He saw that he wasn't the only one who had found some coins in his pocket.

Unlike Nelson, the thug hadn't contemplated or worried about the deeper meaning behind their placement. Oh no, like the practical man that he is, Bradley had simply constructed a set of knuckle-dusters using the coins and some strips of his own shirt. Apart from the brilliances of his single-minded approach, what astounded Nelson more than anything was he hadn't even noticed Bradley constructing it.

"Move out of the way."

"Wait a minute, Bradley. Even with that, you're still going to cause some damage to your fingers. You're not Superman."

"True, but then it isn't stone, just looks like it." Bradley gently pushed Nelson to the side and smacked his fist against the surface.

He wondered if Dane and the charlatan were having as much fun as him. Nelson found that his obsessive worrying over those damn coins had lifted now that he'd discovered that he hadn't been the only one burdened with them. The surface had started to crack. With each punch, more and more cracks spidered out from the centre.

Nelson placed his own fingers against the wall and felt for anything that might give more evidence to either another artificial stone or something else which could point to a way out of there. He should have adopted Bradley's position concerning their predicament from the beginning instead of relying on simply thinking their way out of here. After all, his huge intellect hadn't exactly been of any great service.

"Done it!" he announced. Bradley removed his hand and rubbed his bleeding knuckles against the palm of his other hand. "Hello? Is there anybody in there?"

Both he and Nelson jumped when a pair of eyes appeared in the small gap.

"Got anything shiny?" uttered a high-pitched voice.

"Excuse me?" Nelson leaned over. "Look, can you get us out of here? See if there's a button, a lever, or anything else on your side."

"Yeah, like a door handle," said Bradley.

The eyes blinked. "Shiny thing first, otherwise Branch goes home, has food, has a nap, then comes back when you two little blokes are dead."

"The watch, Nelson, give him the watch."

He pushed his hand into his pocket and brought out the coins and the watch. After a moment's hesitation, Nelson dropped everything back into his pocket save for one coin. He placed that on the top of the stone. A huge hand, twice the size of his, squeezed through the gap and flicked the coin backwards into the darkness.

"I think we've just met Charon," whispered Nelson.

"That's not a lass."

He shook his head in disdain. "You're unbelievable. Bradley, you have spent your career around archaeologists, and you don't know about the ferryman of Hades who transported the new souls across the River Styx?"

"I can drive a car, but that doesn't mean I know the inner workings of the internal combustion engine. I generally tune out when you guy go all technical."

The dark eyes appeared in the gap again. "You've made *Branch* happier. Good job. Hang onto your balls while I sort you out."

"Why does he talk with a crap Australian accent?"

"Like I know the answer to that, Bradley?" He stood back when he heard the sound of huge stones grinding together. His heart sped at the sight of dislodged dust drifting down from the ceiling. Nelson tightened his fists and tried to remain calm and not cry out, despite believing that, at any second, that ceiling was about to start lowering.

"Bloody hell, look at that, it's moving."

Bradley was right, the wall in front of them had begun to slide back. His relief was short lived as his worse fear had also surfaced. The roof was moving as well! The bodyguard grabbed Nelson's wrist and pulled him towards the widening gap. So far, only a couple of inches was visible, whereas the ceiling was dropping at a much faster rate.

At five inches, the wall stopped, but the ceiling continued to descend. Nelson bit his bottom lip to stop him from crying out. Oh God, this was worse than the Yeti mess up!

"One coin isn't going to cut it, I'll need more shiny things or Branch leaves the blokes and comes back when you're as flat as bat shit."

Nelson thrust his hand into his pocket and brought out the rest of the coins. Before he could throw them into the gap, Bradley's hand grabbed his wrist again. The bodyguard shook his head then placed his finger over his lips before Nelson could protest.

He took off his knuckle duster and held it in front of the gap. Three huge fingers appeared out of the other side and tried to snatch it out of Bradley's hand. The bodyguard moved it out of his reach then pressed the wooden shaft against the fingers, pinning them to the stone. "We might end up flat, but you're going to lose your digits as well, my friend."

"Get off me, you ain't supposed to do stuff like that. It's not how it goes."

"Let us out and I'll give you the rest of the coins." Bradley winked at Nelson. "We also have a watch. A really pretty one, really shiny."

How could he remain so calm? That roof was getting lower and lower. It had now reached the stone monoliths. Nelson did release a tiny yelp when he saw the ceiling continue to descend. How was that even possible?

"It's an optical illusion," he replied. "Some kind of projection. It isn't even bloody real." Nelson listened to the man on the other side of that wall curse, then apologise before resorting to cursing again when Bradley refused to move the stick. That guy certainly believed that ceiling wasn't an illusion. Nelson pressed his back against the wall and continued to watch that ceiling, pretend or otherwise coming closer and closer. The two of them continued to argue and beg. The ironic thing was that all he had to do right now was stand up and reach up. He'd be able to tell straight away if it was fake or not. "What if it wasn't?" Nelson growled at the bodyguard. "Just give him what he wants!"

Nelson cried out in relief when the wall started to slide back. He ran over to the widening gap and pushed his body through before collapsing on the other side. As soon as his heart no longer wanted to jump out of his mouth, Nelson slowly raised his gaze from the floor. He nodded at Bradley before looking across at the chamber they'd just left. The wall was already sliding back but there was enough light to show Nelson that Bradley's stick had snapped into two pieces. So much for that ceiling being a projection. He swallowed hard before looking at their reluctant rescuer. The man was too busy running his thick fingers across Bradley's knuckle-duster to notice he was being studied.

Was this another one of the elusive Nephilim? Somehow, he had expected a tall, thick-set, scaled up version of a human. This chap reminded him of a surrealist's interpretation of the classic fairy tale troll who lived under a bridge. The body proportions suggested that he shared more of his DNA to a gorilla than to a man. It didn't make any sense. The female in the photograph looked just like a human female, only much larger. The image was too blurry to make out her face, but he assumed that it wouldn't be too different to a human.

Nelson looked away when the creature jerked his head up.

"What's with the looking, little man? Branch ain't too fond of you little guys, staring. It makes me kinda mad." He shuffled towards Nelson. "That's ain't a great place to live, if you know what I mean. If you don't know, best to keep your eyes off my body, you understand?"

Nelson slowly nodded. "Sorry, I don't want to offend. It's just, well, it's that I've not seen your type before."

"Ain't likely to either. You guys going to tell me what you want? Branch has his shiny things now wants a nap." He paused. "Not all shiny things though." He lumbered a little closer to Nelson. "I could help you out, if you give me the watch."

"What watch?"

"The other guy is a bit handy, ain't scared of me. You though," the giant smiled, revealing a set of grey chisel teeth, "you're a bit of a pudding, and I reckon tastes as good as one too."

He had no idea if this abomination was joking. Nelson took the watch out of his pocket and dropped it into the huge hand that had unfurled before him. The hand was big enough to cover Nelson's face. Imagining those big fingers tightening around his skull made his bowels loosen.

"We want you to help us find our friends, big guy." Bradley pulled Nelson onto his feet and pulled him away from the giant. "Branch, that's your name, right? Well, I think you've had quite enough shiny things from us. Why don't you show a bit of consideration and help us? Do you know where they are?"

He nodded. "Sure I do. Branch knows lots of things." He looked at Nelson. "Branch knows all about you too, Mr. *I'm an important guy because I work for The Trust*. To me though, you'll always be a pudding."

CHAPTER EIGHT

He listened with half an ear as his companion recounted his heroic exploits in the heart of the Madagascar rain forest. Dane had found it increasingly difficult to separate fact from fiction about an hour ago. It just made better sense not to listen to anymore of Benedict's words. He had enough on his plate without having to listen to the other man's insufferable chatter.

Unless his sense of direction was wrong, then the pair of them were walking further and further from his two friends. Dane felt responsible for their disappearance. He didn't think he'd be able to live with himself if anything happened to them. It didn't make any difference that, in reality, Dane had nothing to do with their separation, nor the fact that Bradley was perfectly capable of handling himself. Come to think of it, Nelson had been in more than a few near fatal scrapes.

"That is rather peculiar. See how the markings on the wall to the left of you, Dane, have altered. We now have several groupings of random shapes." He turned to face Dane. "Do you have any explanation?"

Dane shook his head while trying not to berate himself for not paying attention to their surroundings. The fault lay with Benedict and his incessant chattering. He had a vocal tone that could put screaming babies to sleep. "They could be signposts, directing the traveller to their intended destination." The old man nodded slowly. The disguised smirk plastered over Benedict's face did not go unnoticed. Was he making fun of Dane? Or just silently annoyed that Dane had an answer? "It could mean nothing as well." He patted his fingers against the wall. "As we have no other choice than to keep travelling in this direction, I suggest we do that."

"Why not indeed?"

He was, the older man was implying something! Before Dane had a chance to grab him and demand an explanation, Benedict was already over a dozen steps in front of him. Dane had to jog to catch up to him. "What the hell is wrong with—?"

Benedict slapped his large hand across Dane's mouth. "Quiet!" With his other arm, he pointed to his right.

Dane removed the man's hand. He followed Benedict's pointed finger and noticed a narrow intersection. A gap just wide enough to allow one man to squeeze through. "A way out?" he hissed.

"You tell me, Dane." Benedict offered the man a sly grin. "Maybe there's a surprise waiting in there too? I mean, that's how this is supposed to work, is it not?"

"I really have no idea what you are talking about." His next words were left unsaid when his ears picked up the sound of footsteps. "Wait, can you hear that?"

Benedict nodded. "It's why I stopped."

Dane took out his torch and shone the beam against the wall, sliding the light along the stone until it reached the gap. He kept the beam steady and crept a little closer, watching as the torch picked out more detail. "Is there somebody in there?"

The closer he got to the gap, the more convinced Dane was that someone or something was hiding in there. Dane stopped dead when he heard scraping. It sounded like the end of a metal stick running across the stones.

"I'm not sure that this is a good idea, Dane."

The man's sudden air of arrogance was nowhere to be seen. Dane ignored him anyway. He hadn't any idea what had brought upon Benedict's sudden outburst of smugness, not that he cared about the man's bee in his bonnet.

He lowered the light beam, his heartbeat starting to speed up when the torch picked out a clump of feathers. "Oh shit," he muttered as the light settled on the evil-looking eyes of another terror bird. Dane backed away, keeping the torch light fixed upon the creature's thickset body. Was it stuck in there? "Benedict, I think we're all right. I don't believe it can move." The other archaeologist had already left him. The dark was already swallowing up the man's back and heels. "You bloody coward," he spat. Dane turned back around and yelped. The bird was trying to pull itself free! The sight of a prospective meal must have rekindled the bird's will to survive. It had already moved a couple of inches towards Dane.

He played the light over the floor, looking for a rock large enough to bash in the bird's skull. He saw nothing larger than a marble. Dane moved further away, keeping the light fixed on that entrance. When the bird's head jutted out of the intersection and released a terrifying squawk, Dane spun around and raced along the corridor, now eager to catch up with Benedict.

Another screech blasted down the corridor. It sounded to Dane like a screech of triumph. When he heard the bird's galloping feet, he knew he was right. Dane willed his legs to go faster, knowing that it was now just behind him. He shone the light in front of him and finally saw the older archaeologist. He was facing Dane, with his hands on his hips. What the hell was he playing at? Dane then saw the chasm. A gap of about five feet of nothing separating him and Benedict.

He had no other choice. Dane swallowed down the terror, preparing himself before he leapt. The other side was slightly higher. Even so, Dane was still confident that he would be able to make the jump. His first foot touched the lip and he jumped, only for the terror bird's beak to catch the bottom of Dane's trousers.

Screaming, Dane slammed into the side of the rock, the tips of his fingers managing to catch the other edge of the rock.

He felt the sharp stone biting into his skin. He gritted his teeth against the searing pain while listening to the frustrated howl of that nightmarish creature behind him, still trying to get to him. Dane looked up, past his bleeding fingers, to find Benedict staring down at him. What the hell was he doing just looking at him like that? "Help me up, for crying out loud. I don't know how long I can hold on for."

The man got down on his knees and wrapped his thick fingers around Dane's wrists. "Okay," he said slowly. "You can let go now. I've got you."

Dane didn't believe a word. That face suggested that as soon as he did remove his fingers, Benedict was going to drop him. Yet, he knew his grip on the stone was already slipping. His blood had seen to that. "Pull me up, please!"

The older archaeologist looked around the walls, as if looking for something. He then did something that made Dane doubt the man's sanity. He winked at the bird before sticking out his tongue.

"Up you get," he said before dragging Dane up.

He didn't start to relax until his knees were on the ground. Dane rolled away from the edge. He tucked his fingers under his armpits before opening his eyes. "Thank you."

Benedict simply nodded before standing over him. He walked over to the edge and waved at the furious bird. "You can stop your shouting, birdy. Go back where you came from. Go on, bugger off!"

"I don't think it can understand English, Benedict. If anything, you're just making it more upset." Dane got to his feet and examined his sore fingers. The damage wasn't as bad as he'd initially feared. A hot bath and a scotch would soon have them back on the road to recovery. "Come on, let's see where this goes."

The other archaeologist looked directly at him. He opened his mouth and muttered something, but the noise from the terror bird drowned out his words. Dane leaned against the wall. He had no idea what had got into the man. Dane was about to confront him, to find out exactly what his problem was, when the wall behind Dane shifted. "What the hell?" Dane spun around and watched in horror as what he previously believed to be a jutting-out rock, slid into the stone.

"What have you done now?" Benedict jumped towards him. "Oh, you bloody shit. I knew I should have…" Benedict ran past Dane.

He stepped away from the wall, his mouth drying up when he saw a wide stone platform sliding out from the stone face, heading towards the other side of the path, towards the waiting bird. "That's so not fair," he shouted while scrambling after Benedict. He raced down the dark corridor while listening to the huge claws on the bird's feet crack against the floor. He should have just gone into that narrow gap while he could and just throttled the bloody thing.

Benedict was just in front of him, but it looked as though he was slowing down. Dane caught up to the older archaeologist and found they'd reached another junction. This time, there were four more corridors, all of them narrow.

"What the hell do we do now?" screamed Benedict. "All of them are going to contain one of those birds, I just know it."

Dane looked the way they came and saw that their pursuer had slowed down. He looked at Benedict then at each of those entrances in front of them. He didn't need to possess Benedict's superior sense of hearing to know that the other man was right. "There must be another way out of here. There has to be!" Dane rubbed his hands along the walls, trying to find another hidden lever that might open up another safe way out of there. His searching fingers found no levers, but they did expose some more geometric shapes.

"Why has it stopped, Dane? What's going to happen now?"

"Will you stop that? How am I supposed to know what's going to happen? There's no agenda here, no script."

"Are you sure about that? Because I'm not sure that I believe you."

Dane just shook his head; he had more important things to worry about. For a start, he was now very much aware of movement coming from those other narrow tunnels. His fore finger fell into a shallow groove. His finger moved along the groove, only stopping when the tip smacked against a dome-shaped point.

"Interesting," he said.

"Oh no! There's four of them now. No, make that six. Look at the bloody size of them!"

Dane rested his finger on the stone button, uttered a silent prayer, then pushed it in. A section of wall a couple of feet from the floor slowly slid upwards, revealing a rectangular patch of total blackness. Before Dane had time to express surprise, Benedict climbed inside and threw himself forward.

The sight of seven huge birds racing towards him took away any hesitation. Dane jumped into the gap and screamed out in shock as a chute slid him down to some unknown destination.

A mountainous pile of brittle bones broke his fall. Dane tumbled and rolled. He tucked his arms and legs into his body and held closed his mouth to stop himself from breathing in the choking dust. Finally, the inertia slowed and he came to a halt beside Benedict's feet. Dane gazed in awe at the vast size of this cavern, as well as the sheer amount of animal remains in here. The entrance to the chute was way up at the top of this cavern. "There's no way we're going to leave that way," he muttered. Dane reckoned that the pair of them must have dropped over a thousand metres.

He slowly got to his feet while instinctively checking his body for anything broken. Dane was sore in a few places, but he'd come out of it relatively intact. He was about to ask Benedict if he was okay when the other men grabbed his hair and viciously pulled his head back. Before Dane could respond, he felt the razor-sharp edge of a long blade pressed against his throat.

"Time for some answers, Dane," he snarled.

"Get off me, you idiot!"

"Start with what the game is." He leaned closer. "I can't see any cameras in here, so I'm guessing we must be out of their vision." Benedict pressed the knife a little harder. "That's good, really. It means I can do this without any of your mates sounding the alarm. Don't worry, as soon as you do tell me what I want to know, I'll move us towards a camera so your mates can rescue us."

The blade had broken the skin. Dane felt his hot blood streaming down his skin. It didn't hurt, not yet. What the hell was this fool going on about? What cameras? He took a deep breath, desperately trying to stay calm, to stop his anger from boiling over. Whether he wanted to admit it, Dane needed to keep this idiot alive, even if he had begun to lose his marbles.

"I guess there's no point in denying the cameras," he replied.

"So, I was right about you. I knew it!"

The pressure eased off just a bit. Dane eased his body closer to Benedict. "Did you notice them right from the start?"

"No, not at first. It's only when the spiders moved along the ceiling. One of their legs dislodged some webbing. Your torchlight reflected from a lens. That was a stupid thing to do, Dane. I guess you must have forgotten where you put that one. Still, these things happen."

Benedict had no time to engage in another gloating revelation as Dane slammed the back of his head into the bridge of the older man's nose. He then grabbed Benedict's wrist and twisted it around, not stopping until he heard the knife clattering on the floor. Dane pushed the man back, scooped up the knife, and stepped back holding the weapon in front of him. "Listen to me, you silly old bastard! I don't have a clue what you're talking about. I know nothing about any cameras, nor do I know why we are down here!"

"I don't believe you."

Dane wiped his fingers across his throat. He couldn't tell whether the blood on his skin was from his throat or his previous wounds. "Do you think I care what you think?" He paused. "You were going to drop me. I don't believe this. You really were going to let me fall to my death just because you thought I might have had something to do with what's happened to us?"

"What else did you expect?"

"I expected you to trust me," he screamed. "What, you think we're in some television game show, that a live audience is betting on who live or dies? That there are fabulous prizes to be won?" He picked up one of the bones and threw it at Benedict. "That all this is pretend." He slid the knife into the back of his trousers and walked away from the other man. "Perhaps, those birds are fake too." He turned and sneered at Benedict. "Perhaps it's just a man in a costume."

"Where are you going?"

Dane didn't stop walking. "Away from you."

He could hear the other man following him but didn't turn around. Dane no longer cared about him anymore. He kept his eyes fixed on the distant ceiling. There were more than one chute leading down here to the floor. Enormous piles of bones surrounded their exits. As Dane moved from one to the other, he saw the bones were getting fresher, as evidenced by the stench emanating from the piles. He had to lift his jacket and hold it over his mouth and nose before continuing.

"Some of these bones look human," replied Benedict. "Plus, I think there is at least one other human-like species."

Dane ignored the man. He'd already seen two human skulls lying at the bottom of a bone pile. What caught Dane's eye was the sight of what looked like an exit, about half a mile from where they stood. To get to the exit involved climbing over some of the fresher piles of dismembered carcasses.

"Look, I'm sorry, Dane. I was wrong about you. I apologise."

"This must be what happened to the remains of the terror bird's meals." Dane turned around, looking past Benedict's imploring face and gazed back at the chute that had dropped the pair of them in here. That was the first one and, he guessed, the oldest. It's entirely possible that he and Benedict were that chute's unwilling passengers in over a few dozen thousand years, back when those murderous animals actually roamed the land above.

"Tell me when you stopped seeing the cameras," he said abruptly. "I bet you still haven't seen any in here, and don't lie to me by telling me you haven't been looking."

"I haven't seen any cameras since we were separated from the others, but that doesn't mean they're not up there somewhere. Look, can I have my knife back, please? I feel naked without it."

Dane shook his head. "I'll think about it. Where did you find the knife? My assumption was that we were all searched before waking up down here. Did you pick it up on our journey?"

Benedict shook his head. "It isn't mine, but I did find the article upon my person, a few moments after opening my eyes."

There wouldn't be any more cameras. That much, Dane did know. He crouched down and brushed aside enough bones to allow him to sit on the floor. "Benedict, we are both scientists, in a sense. We might not wear the lab coats, but our thought processes still mirror our cousins in the labs." He sighed heavily and glared at the other man. "Do you agree?"

"Well, yes. I guess so."

Dane pulled out the knife and tossed it towards Benedict's feet. "So, if I was complicit in this abduction, I would give you a weapon?"

"But the patterns. You solved them with ease!"

"And that makes me suspect? If your mind hadn't been full of your paranoid fantasy, I know you would have arrived at the solution before me. Benedict, you can stop looking for the cameras. There won't be any down here."

"How can you be so sure?"

He tapped the floor. "Because we are the first ones to set foot in here. This is the equivalent of Neil Armstrong setting foot on the moon."

"But—"

"No buts. I'm right about this. You see, whoever discovered this place was only able to explore the tip of the iceberg. To go further required the expertise of some very specific individuals."

Benedict picked up the knife. "I suddenly feel very foolish. Why didn't they just ask us?"

"Unknown. I would have jumped at the chance to explore this place. It is one of the questions I intend to pose once we find our companions."

"Wait, you know what this is?"

Dane motioned Benedict to join him before he wiped away a section of thick dust in front of his knee. "I wish I had my brush," he muttered. Dane grinned at what his fingers had uncovered. "Isn't it interesting?" He glanced at Benedict's shocked face. "Do you not think that it's a little grandiose to have this magnificent and intricate mosaic tile floor under a waste collection area?" Dane brushed away more of the debris. "My guess is this was once used as a theatre or debating hall, or whatever analogous concept the species used in their society. The chutes and subsequent animal waste are a result of some unforeseen catastrophe."

He stood and helped Benedict up. "We have discovered a Nephilim city." Dane held up his hand. "Remove that incredulous look from your face, Benedict. Nelson and I were already on our way to investigate rumours of giant humans before our unfortunate apprehension."

"This could be the greatest discovery of the millennium. If, of course, you're right."

"I am right," replied Dane. He lowered his voice. "Of course, we still have to find details of them and our friends. Not to mention find a way out of here and get home before the ones who shot down my plane turn up."

Benedict shrugged. "We had better get a move on then."

CHAPTER NINE

A single drop of Nelson's sweat fell from his forehead and landed in the middle of the huge spider's back. It took every strength of his being to fight the overwhelming instinct to scream and stamp on the vile animal. As instructed, he stayed totally still, only shifting his eyeballs a fraction until Bradley's serene features swam into view.

The bodyguard responded to Nelson's silent plea for help with a brief shake of his head. Oh Jesus, two more of the horrible hairy bastards were now crawling along the stone ledge, heading straight for his other boot.

"Kill the bloody thing!" he hissed. "Do it now before his pals get any closer and start to have a party." This was just unbelievable. The bodyguard's idiotic grin had yet to leave that gormless face. It was all right for him to look so smug and superior; he didn't have an eight-legged monster making its way towards his tender ankle!

"If you move even an inch, Nelson, those spiders eating into your leg will be the last thing on your mind." His grin grew wider. "Move and I'll bury my fists in your face."

There were another three spiders heading towards him now! Nelson didn't know what to do. As much as he mentally berated the thug and thought Bradley was missing a few brain cells, Nelson didn't doubt the man wouldn't honour his threat.

This just wasn't fair. Having his face shoved in seconds before a swarm of spiders turned him into burger meat was not how he expected to end his existence! The thug's savage threat did the trick, though. Nelson didn't move a muscle. The sheer idea of Bradley's hard fists breaking his face utterly terrified him. He looked away from the bodyguard's glower and found his gaze drifting down to his feet, only to discover that the spider had already moved away from his foot. In fact, they were all crawling up the side of the walls. His eyes followed the lead arachnid, not daring to breathe until its disgusting body and legs had vanished from sight.

Nelson quietly gasped when Bradley grabbed his upper arm and jerked him away from the crawling column of arachnids.

"It was the lead one we needed the keep an eye on, the spider exploring your foot. That's the head honcho, you see. Old Sam spider is like a scout or something, but more than that, I reckon that fellow's venom contains a chemical, a pheromone. Once its fangs break the skin, that chemical sends all the others into a total frenzy."

Benedict felt physically sick.

"They're not normal spiders. That much I do know. Then again, what is normal around here?"

"Why didn't you just say that right at the beginning when we first saw that spider?"

Bradley shrugged. "The way I figured it, you didn't listen to me when I said we should have stayed where Branch left us, so why should you listen to me now?" Bradley winked at Nelson before spinning around and walking off.

Perhaps if he hadn't been so preoccupied with the damn coins, Nelson might have noticed their unusual behaviour. It would have been right at the beginning, not long after their awakening. While he and the others were quietly panicking over their situation, David Attenborough over there was scrutinising those bloody spiders.

Nelson gripped the side of his thighs to try to ease the shaking. He watched the thug head back towards that overhanging rock. He cut a fine figure of a man. Cool, calm, and collected, just as he was when Nelson watched those spiders take that poor man apart.

He took a deep shaking breath before rushing after the bodyguard, while vaguely wondering if the thug had taken notes.

"How are you holding up, Nelson? You don't look too good."

Was he making fun of him? "I've had better days," he replied. It did occur to him that Bradley, the great white hunter, might not be far from the mark with his rather demeaning observation. Nelson hadn't been feeling himself for quite some time now, ever since he woke up in this place, to be honest.

For a start, since when was he ever scared of a few spiders, poisonous or otherwise? Oh, there had been more than a few moments in his career when the appearance of those eight-legged bastards had turned the inside of his mouth into the bottom of a canary cage. Nelson had never been too keen of them as a species. There was something about the way they moved and the appearance of all those fine hairs covering far too many legs that put the wind up him. Even so, due to his choice of work, you just had to accept the dangers and general shiver factor of bumping into spiders, as well as the thousands of other creepy-crawlies which accompanied them.

He remembered that occasion four years ago, when that colony of African hunting spiders invaded his camp-site. That was certainly a bowel-loosening experience, but even that paled in comparison to how he reacted with the buggers down here. This was 'jumping on a stool, pulling up his skirt, and screaming like a big girl' kind of emotion.

Obsessing over those damn coins was another aberration to his, what he believed to be, stable persona. Why should he even care if the coins held some deeper relevance? The chap running this circus probably only popped them in there to mess with his head.

"It obviously worked then, you silly old fool," he muttered.

Nelson had always been so proud of being able to think his way out of any tricky situation. Applying cold, hard logic coupled with his extensive experience, made for such a formidable partnership.

He looked over at Bradley, standing with his left leg casually resting on a rocky outcrop, looking like some full-sized Action Man, with the emphasis on *Man*. Nelson got the distinct feeling that Bradley believed he was the alpha, while poor Nelson was the bumbling sidekick. He sighed to himself, while grinding his teeth in annoyance. There was still plenty of time to burst that ugly bubble.

Right now, Nelson needed to get back into his mind-set and to focus on what he knew about these giants. After all, despite the opinions of others, it would be Nelson who'd be bringing this particular adventure to a satisfactory conclusion. There was nobody on the planet who knew more about these elusive creatures than him now that the weird feeling had finally departed. It was time to put all that knowledge to good use.

Nelson lowered his body onto the dry cavern floor, while trying not to break out in a fit of hysterical giggling. Put his vast knowledge to good use, did he really think that?

The total sum of factual information regarding these giant humans could have fit into two pages from a small notepad. Rumours about them, stories, myths and legends, well, there was enough of that rubbish to fill a library.

There was one particular theme which did run through the more credible stories, rumours, and legends, and that was that these giants built a gleaming city which stood for thousands of years. They stripped it and vanished underground before the first human even landed on the southern continent. This obviously begged the question of how we even knew about this supposed race of giant humans. The answers ranged from the first people finding remains to a small group of giants electing to stay behind.

It seemed inconceivable that the giants were still around when the first people did appear on the scene. After all, they had the home ground, stronger, more numerous, and were obviously far more technologically advanced.

Nelson thought back to Bradley's question about normality. Perhaps that was the key. Perhaps the spiders were not a natural product but a genetically altered animal, just like those huge birds. The giants had employed them to act as guardians to prevent anybody from ever finding them.

What kind of mind-set did it take to choose to hide instead of fighting? Could the giant really be free of any aggression? That they were a true race of pacifists? That manic who had kidnapped them would go wild if that really was the case.

He caught up with Bradley, idly wondering why he had never pursued this line of reasoning before.

"I know this is going to sound like an odd question, Bradley."

"Like that's ever stopped you before."

Nelson bit his tongue and swallowed down his immediate retort. "You mentioned that the spiders weren't normal. In what way?"

The bodyguard shook his head. "Dunno, like they're a new

species or something."

Nelson nodded to himself. His idea of the giant engineering the spiders took hold and refused to move. Was it really beyond the realms of scientific plausibility that this couldn't happen?

"One more question. How did you feel when you woke up inside those caverns? I mean, did you feel any ill effects from whatever they used on us?"

"You sure are asking a lot of questions lately." He sighed loudly. "No, I didn't suffer any ill effects."

There probably wasn't that much in that head to ruin. The ape obviously only operated on instinct and response.

Now that his senses were clear, Nelson was certain of one overriding factor.

"Bradley, there's no way we can stay here. I wouldn't trust that deformed freak as far as I could throw him."

"You sure do have an annoying habit of stating the obvious," replied Bradley. "Believe me, I'm fully aware of our situation, but unless you can come up with an alternate course of action, we have no other choice but to stay put."

Bradley leaned forward and lightly tapped the side of Nelson's head. "Come on, Brain Box. Tell me what all those weird symbols cut into the rock means."

Nelson couldn't answer the man. He didn't have a single idea.

"It's pretty obvious to me that our funky-looking pal knows this place like the back of his deformed hand."

"Okay then, what do you suggest?"

"We simply treat this as an information gathering exercise until we know more about our new friend and his plans. There's nothing else we can do."

"Speak of the devil," hissed Nelson. The man or whatever the hell he was, had just lumbered around the corner, waving his usual guilty-looking smirk

"I hope you two fellas have behaved yourselves." Branch released a high-pitched giggle which sounded totally odd for a creature of his size.

"Oh, you know. Here and there. There and here. Mostly there." Branch's jovial expression suddenly darkened. "Right. If the pair of you worms have stopped bloody interrogating me like the sets of bastards that you are, I've found some guy who'll help you out." He then pointed to a light-grey flat rock close to where Nelson stood. "You two fellas are going to follow me now." He grinned. "And if you see me pointing like I am now, you need to do everything you can to avoid standing or touching it. You get me?"

He waited until both men nodded before turning back around and racing off down the narrow cavern tunnel.

Nelson took the lead, doing his best to keep up with Branch's long paces.

After a couple of minutes, Branch skidded to a stop. He stepped to the left and pointed to a small, black sharp rock, jutting out of the side of the wall opposite him.

"That's a good one, fellas. Get too close to that bad boy and the whole section of cavern falls away." He chuckled. "There's a huge nest of hungry birds right under you two. If you listen hard enough, you might even hear those monsters fussing. I tell you, they're so eager to rip the sweet meat from your tiny bones."

"Okay," said Bradley. "You've made your point."

"Okay yourself, squirt. I'm only trying to look out for you fellas. I mean, I didn't ask you to come nosing down here, sticking your nose in where it has no business."

Branch spun around and carried on walking down the cavern tunnel. "Any more back chatter from the likes of you and I might not tell you about the next trap. We'll see how you like those bananas."

Nelson struggled to keep up with their reluctant guide. He guessed that Bradley wanted to give Branch a slap for that rather nasty retort. He didn't care about any of that, he was too busy thinking about how a bunch of peace-loving benevolent creatures would devise a trap that killed their intruders in such a horrific way.

If the giants were so concerned about conserving life, then wouldn't they create a labyrinth which led the intruders back the way they came? He stopped dead, narrowly avoiding Bradley bumping into him. Nelson allowed the bodyguard to pass him while he glanced across at that black rock.

Who's to say that they weren't originally designed like that?

Hell, it's quite possible that these caverns are four times older than the great Egyptian pyramids. In all those untold thousands of years, anybody could have altered this labyrinth. That freaky Branch guy couldn't have been the only specimen to set up home down here.

Which brought Nelson back to his initial argument with Nelson. Who's to say that Branch wasn't leading them into a situation worse than the one they were already in? His hand drifted into his pocket and he found himself playing with that stupid coin yet again. He whipped his hand out of the pocket and threw the bloody coin in the general direction of that rock before turning around and running towards the others.

Bradley was right. What other choice did they have? They had no option but to keep going even if that bastard was leading them to their doom, like some kind of genetically deformed pied piper.

It didn't take long to catch up with the pair of them as they had both stopped moving. Branch's fingers danced across two rows of patterns embossed into the side of the rock as just as before, he had that annoying smirk plastered over his ugly face.

Nelson felt the bodyguard's hand grip his arm at the same time as the cavern wall began to slide back. Bradley tried to pull him away from the giggling hybrid, but his efforts were hampered by several men rushing through the opening gap. They forcefully dragged Bradley over to Branch, who casually put the bodyguard on the floor.

Nelson slowly turned to find a very familiar face glaring at him.

"You are such a chump!" snarled Marlon. "How could you allow the other two to get away? Thanks to you, we've lost all contact of them. I am so upset with you right now. Upset enough to have both of you fed to the pairs, feet first." He paused. "Unless, of course, you are able to take us straight to them?"

Nelson tore his gaze away from Marlon. He took one look at Bradley before he finally allowed his gaze to settle on the still grinning face of Branch.

"I think you already know the answer to that one, Marlon. Like we know where the hell they are."

"Yes, thought not. Well, it's been nice knowing you, Nelson. Sorry, but I can't let you wander around here, you know how it is."

Nelson's grin now matched the one still stuck to the hybrid. "Hold your horses, young man. I bet your deformed pet could take you straight to Dane and Benedict." Judging from the look of astonishment, that made a brief appearance on that sly face, Nelson had guessed right.

"Is this true?" asked Marlon.

Branch nodded. "Sure, I could take you guys there," he replied. "Only, what do I get in return?" His eyes scanned Marlon's assembled heavies before he stopped at the brute currently holding Bradley's neck. Nelson did find it rather amusing to watch one action man assault another action man.

"I really like his boots," he giggled. "I really do like his boots."

Nelson's amusement only grew at the sight of Marlon's crumpled up face when he realised just how stupid he had been.

"That must really grate you. I mean, you must have spent ages tracking us down, when all you had to do was to give your monkey a pair of boots."

Voicing aloud the man's mess-up probably wasn't the best idea that he'd had all day, not knowing how dangerously unstable he was, but it would but worth it just to see if Marlon blew a gasket.

"I'm so happy that you're enjoying my discomfort, Nelson. I still have no reason to keep you two alive."

"I don't think Dane will be happy to hear that you killed his mate. I wouldn't be too trusting in your new pet either, even if you do give him the boots. He's about as trustworthy as you are."

"You!" he snarled. "Give him your boots." Marlon glanced up at Branch. "Looks like the ball's in your court, my friend. Lead the way. Just remember. If you try to trick us, the next shiny things you'll be seeing are a spread of bullets stitched across your chest."

Nelson found himself and Bradley sandwiched between two of Marlon's heavies.

"Thanks for that," hissed Bradley.

He simply nodded. *Brains over brawn* had triumphed again.

CHAPTER TEN

Any word, simple or complex, could not describe the turmoil of volatile emotions currently running riot inside his aching head.

Marlon thrust his hands deep into his pockets. It was the safest place for them. Otherwise, he could see himself snatching a weapon from the nearest guard and killing every single one of these duplicitous people. Marlon would take great pleasure in reducing Dane's smug face into a stamped-on blood pie. In fact, he might even make all the others, the ones who were all silently mocking him, eat a slice. That would teach them.

He'd have to shoot him in the kneecap first, just to stop him laughing at poor Marlon. Marlon didn't even need to turn around to know that the man was laughing at him.

It wasn't just Dane, either. That old man obviously thought he'd got away with making him look like a fool in front of the others. Yeah, well, Mr. Clever Nelson, just like the others, you would end up dead, just not yet though. Not until he had got what exactly what he wanted.

The first one here to get what he deserved, just had to be that freak. Marlon intended to torture and kill that Branch, not because he couldn't be trusted, or that something that grotesque should have been drowned at birth. Not even because he wouldn't stop staring in lust at Marlon's slave. He was going to hurt the freak just on general principle.

It had been a full hour since the altercation with Nelson and twenty minutes since locating Dane and Benedict. Marlon thought that by now the anger should have, at least, lessened; not to utterly dissipate, as the days when Marlon didn't feel constantly angry were as rare as rocking-horse shit these days.

The fury just didn't sit right. What was wrong with him? Considering his recent achievements, Marlon should at least be able to crack one smile. He had done it, He's battled against the insurmountable odds and still came out on top. Was it worry or perhaps something else, another particular deviant flaw of his personality which refused to leave him alone?

He had ordered Dane and Benedict to walk in front, to keep an eye on them. Those were the exact words he'd used, much to the amusement of Marlon's associates. They deserved to be treated like children in his eyes.

Marlon listened to Dane discussing theories and ideas with Benedict like this was a normal bloody expedition, that Marlon hadn't kidnapped them, like they weren't in danger. Marlon ground his teeth. Like he didn't even exist.

He gripped the fabric inside his pockets and willed himself to calm down. They weren't ignoring him at all, he was just really, really worried that something was going to go wrong just as he was this close to achieving his ultimate goal. Of course, they weren't excluding him on purpose. This wasn't like those hurtful times back when Marlon was a child and his older brother and father used to purposely ignore him by either shutting off their conversation whenever he entered their sphere of influence or when they even turned their back on him.

The two archaeologists were just excited at being able to walk through the find of the millennium, and this really was a sensational discovery. Even if, in the worst possible outcome, he didn't find his race of warrior giants, this alone would ensure that his name lived forever.

A perfectly preserved city of advanced humanoid beings older that known human history would change the world; who knew what treasure lay beneath their feet? Well, those two in front of him might have an idea, but it wasn't like Marlon was able to join in their conversation. He only understood three out of every ten words that came out of their mouths.

Right now, Benedict was arguing that the archaeological style was more of a parallel evolution rather than some kind of indirect influence to ancient classical lines. That although the designs were similar, it was impossible to suggest that there could be a common line due to the separation of time and continents.

Marlon couldn't understand how the threat of death from his

men didn't even raise an eyebrow and yet to suggest that the giants all lived in Ancient Greet temples caused both men to become bitter enemies.

Watching them square up did help him begin to calm down. He had almost reached the point where he felt enough confidence to remove his hands from his pockets when that Dane dropped the ultimate bombshell.

He suggested that the original builders of this forgotten city were pacifists. In fact, both men were convinced of this stupid idea. They even had the audacity to say that Marlon's slave, the way she cowered around him and flinched whenever Marlon rose his voice, wasn't abnormal behaviour, at least, not for her species.

His hand left that pocket, his fingers already tightening on the trigger. He'd shoot just one of them, that's all, just to show these indignant clowns not to mess with him. He didn't need all of them anyway, not now.

Marlon's decision to shoot Nelson in the kneecaps went right out of his head at the sight of his slave walking past the lot of them. For a second, he couldn't even find the words to order her back to her position right behind him. He looked at the others; thankfully, all their eyes were on her as well so they didn't notice the panic that he knew must be showing on his face. He raised his hand. Marlon had to shoot her, he just had to. There's no way he dare order her back to his side. The others would hear the weakness in his voice.

Both Branch and the bodyguard unintentionally put themselves between him and his slave, denying him the shot. He had to put the gun away, otherwise he would have fired and kept firing until he ran out of rounds.

"What is she doing?"

Benedict's question was directed at Nelson, but it was Dane who held up his hand to silence the man. The archaeologist ran over to her, climbed onto a low wall beside the now still giant, and waved his hands across her face. "There's no response," he said.

Marlon pushed himself through them and stood by the wall, looking in confusion at his slave. She didn't even look alive. He almost screamed when the woman suddenly started to quietly laugh. It was probably the most beautiful noise that he had ever heard. Even Branch was caught up in the angelic melody.

"I remember this place," she said, hear voice was barely a whisper. "Oh, I so used to enjoy our trips to the city park. I was small enough to hide in the long grass but tall enough to reach the ripe fruits of the paleberries hanging from the lowest branches in the orchard. We stayed in the park, all the children, while our parents attended the meetings." She began to frown. "The park trips grew ever more frequent." She started to shake. "Until they became every cycle."

Her haunting monologue had transfixed them all, apart from Marlon. He looked around, and he discovered that he wasn't the only one no longer listening to her whining. Dane was a couple of feet away, holding something in his hand.

The gun came back out. Her pointed the dangerous end at the archaeologist and ordered him to pass it over. Dane just shrugged before dropping it into Marlon's outstretched palm. "What is it?"

Dane grinned at him. "If you hadn't snatched it away from me, I might have had enough time to examine it."

"What is it with you? Can you not see the gun in my hand? I mean, it's almost like you want me to pull the trigger. I will, you know. Just you watch me. I have killed before, lots of times, and I…" His words dropped away when he saw that Dane was no longer looking at him. He was staring at the giant. In fact, they all were, and his slave was staring him. She had lost that faraway look and her standard expression of terror had crawled back onto her face once more. He would have taken comfort in this if it wasn't for the fact that he realised that her fear wasn't directed at him, his new acquisition was the cause of her terror.

"Put it on her," said Bradley.

"What?"

"Can't you see what it is?" replied the bodyguard. "They're headphones. Go on, put them on her!"

Comprehension finally dawned. He smiled, then ordered her over to his side. The giant then performed an action that had never happened to him before. She said no and shook her head. This time, nobody was going to stop Marlon from shooting her dead. He raised his gun only to have Branch slap the weapon out of his hand before grabbing the artefact. He ran over to the slave and put the object on the girl's head before anyone could react.

She arched her back and screamed before collapsing. They all ran over to her still body and stood over the woman. It was only the appearance of a grey sphere, the size of a ball-bearing, that caused them to take a couple of paces back. Marlon watched in amazement as the sphere grew larger until it was the size of a small car. It hung, directly under the giant's head. Marlon looked across at Dane who shrugged back. It appeared that even this was beyond anything that he had encountered before.

"I can see something now," said Benedict.

Marlon swallowed his fear and moved a little closer. He now saw a large green area, full of strange-looking trees, with large white buildings behind. The view then spun until Marlon now saw a long, broad walkway, made of a mosaic of coloured, rectangular stone blocks. He looked down and saw the same but faded and cracked blocks below their feet. "This must be what this place once looked like."

"There's movement in there."

He looked up, expecting to see themselves in there. Dane saw movement all right, but it wasn't then. A dark-skinned, well-built man, holding what looked like a blow-pipe, had entered the walkway beside the man.

Beside him, Marlon saw somebody a couple of paces away, only he wore the uniform of some early European soldier.

"Holy shit!" Benedict stared straight at Nelson. "That's a Spanish conquistador!"

Nelson nodded. "I think we might have found out what happened here."

Her eyelids flickered open. It took a couple of moments for the girl's thoughts to catch up with her body. By that time, the warm rays from the city's fusion generator had already started to take away the chill and began to dry out the dew from the grass that had collected on her bare arms and legs.

She couldn't have been asleep for that long. A couple of minutes at the most. Any longer than that and she was sure that somebody would have noticed her sleeping form and woken her. The little girl yawned before slowly sitting up. She rubbed the small of her back while turning to the left and then to the right. This couldn't be right. She couldn't see anybody else in the park, even the two little boys who she had been playing with when her mother first left her had gone too. They told her that the warden had only just finished building a rope swing at the bottom and they intended to be the first people to play on it.

She looked across at the direction the giggling boys had run. She saw the rope swing, but there was no sign of them. Perhaps their mother had taken them home, meaning the meeting must have finished. If that was right then where was her mother? Where was everybody else? These sorts of situations never used to bother her. She, like all her friends and family, took life in their stride, to enjoy your existence was to live it. Stress, fear, and worry belonged in the distant past.

From what she had observed recently, their distant past might have just caught up with them. In the past few cycles, the city meetings had become progressively more frequent. Something was wrong, but because of her young age, nobody would tell her what it was.

In cycles past, she wouldn't have been all that bothered at what the grown-ups did and just carried on as normal. What her body urged her to do right now was to laze about in all this luxurious grass a little longer before skipping down to the orchard to pick some of the ripe fruit hanging from those low branches.

Her wish would not be happening as a barb of uncertainty had just appeared in her guts and whenever she thought about staying here, right away, that barb doubled in size. She just had to try and get into that building or the assembly and see if she could finally discover what the adults were discussing in there.

She ran through the grass and passed all the trees in the orchard, not stopping once, not even to pick that really juicy-looking paleberry, hanging right by her shoulder. Once she reached the edge of the park, she now saw where the two boys had gone. They obviously had the same idea as she did. They were trying to climb onto the roof of the building of the assembly, and failing miserably.

Those idiots were going to hurt themselves. She did not intend to sneak inside. Whatever was happening to the city affected everyone, including her and the two boys. She watched the boys for another moment. Now that her mind was made up, she knew that fruit, the one she ignored, could now be taken.

She waved at the boys, waiting for them to see her before going back into the park to retrieve that paleberry. There's no way that she could leave that just hanging there. Once her prize was in her hands, she jogged out of the park and didn't stop until she reached the front doors of the meeting hall. She looked straight at the boys while taking out a huge bite of the fruit. Their twin looks of disbelief when she walked straight up to the front door so made her smile. It almost made her earlier worry fade into insignificance. Almost.

Without waiting for the boys to catch up, she walked straight through the main doors and made her way down the corridor. She had been here lots of times, but only with her mother. They used to open the meeting place for teaching and games during the holidays. Even so, back then, at least the lights were on at optimum strength. As she slowly walked towards the increasing sound of heated conversation, she so wished that those two boys would catch up with her. The dull lighting began to make her very uneasy.

It took a lot of effort not to gasp out loud when she did reach the perimeter. She had never seen so many people together before. Everybody in the city must be in the meeting hall. It felt so strange

The last time she was in here, she and three other girls played a game of running from one end to the other. It took ages to get from one wall to the other. Now, it would be impossible to move, never mind run about.

There was no sign of her mother. In fact, apart from the backs of the people in front of her, she saw nobody she knew. The voice coming from somewhere at the front came from the mouth of their civic leader. She knew him, but without a face, it sounded so odd, although that might have been because it sounded so sad.

This was a little boring. She was so tempted to go back to the park and wait for all this adult stuff to finish. This thought took hold and she turned around to leave when she caught sight of the two boys sneaking down the corridor. Unlike her, the boys were not so subtle with their movements and voices. The pair of them saw the assembled crowd and let out a frightened squeal, causing the end row to spin around. Even that disembodied voice went silent.

The boys were about to flee when the voice asked some of the adults to bring the children closer. He also asked two more adults to bring the others in here as well.

The crowd parted, and the girl was hushed towards the front where her mother waited. She smiled at the girl before scooping her in her arms and giving her a tight cuddle.

This was so much better that eating paleberries. All that spoiled her perfect moment were so many sad faces.

She hoisted up onto her mother's shoulder where, finally, she saw the civic leader on the stage along with several other solemn-looking men.

Without realising it, that shard of worry had set up a home in her guts. This was bad, really bad.

The civic leader looked directly at her. "Perhaps we should have invited you and your friends right at the beginning?" He then turned to the whole crowd and spread his arms. "My only regret is that we should have reached this decision when the time of the first invasion of the little people. Our ancestors lived in the hope that nature would have realised her mistake and rectified it. That did not come to pass."

"But they're not a problem and maybe these new ones will not stay?"

The civic leader looked straight at the voice in the crowd. "This is the question posed by our ancestors all those thousands of cycles in the past. It is true that the original invaders found their path. The new invaders are too troubled inside. The only path they will follow is one of violence, murder, and destruction." He sighed. "They are now about us and have already begun to look for routes which lead to our city."

A collective groan rose from the crowd when a viewscreen behind the civic leader showed two little people picking their way through one of the caverns. One of them looked just like she imagined little people to look, but the other one wore red fabric and shiny metal plates. One look at the device clasped in his hand told her that this one just had to be evil.

"Our race will be reborn. This our destiny, our purpose."

"Our goal," replied everyone in the assembly room.

She watched everybody slowly walk out if the room. She saw her three friends and she waved. Neither of them waved back.

Before long, only her mother remained. She gently placed the girl back on the floor and crouched in front of her. "Do you understand what is about to happen?"

Hot tears ran down her cheeks. "Will it hurt? I don't want it to hurt."

Her mother shook her head. "Move, you won't feel a thing. You will close your eyes and when you open them, we'll all be together again on the surface, and they'll be no little people and all the paleberries you can eat." Her mother asked her to open her mouth. She placed a small green pill on the tip of the girl's tongue and asked her to swallow it.

Marlon took his eyes off the viewscreen and watched his slave's eyes flicker open. She coughed before slowly sitting up. She pulled the device from her head and threw it behind her.

"Then what happened?"

"The death pill or whatever it was obviously didn't work," snapped Dane while glaring at Marlon.

"I woke up and found myself lying in the middle of the assembly hall," she replied. "The lights were fading. In less than a cycle, only a single emergency light worked. Its dull glow cast everything in a dirty, red light. Even with that single light, I knew that I was alone. Outside the building showed me the same scene. All the people had gone, leaving me in a broken city all in this dull red shadow."

"Wait, what do you mean by broken?"

The giant looked at Nelson. "Nothing worked anymore. In the final order, the civic leader had shut down everything, except for the few remaining lights. They'll stay on for as long as the upworld sun shines."

"So, they're all dead?" asked Marlon.

She nodded. "Yes, they knew that your chaotic and murderous ancestors would stop at nothing to possess what we owned, so the civic leader ensured that all our technology would no longer work before they all committed the final act."

"Jesus," said Bradley. "Talk about overkill. Your people could have wiped them all out without breaking into a sweat, girl. To kill all of yourselves is just," he shook his head in dismay, "it's just a senseless waste."

"Not everything is junk," said Dane. "That thing we put on your head still worked and that device which Nelson had worked too."

The girl nodded. She hung her head. "We obviously weren't as perfect as we chose to believe." She looked straight at Dane, her face crumpled up in misery. "I didn't die like the others and I spend all these thousands of cycles having to live with you violent savages."

"So, they're all dead?" Marlon repeated. He aimed his gun at Nelson. He would be the first one to get it. Marlon had never really liked that one anyway. All gazes were now fixed on his gun, which was exactly how it should be. He licked his lips. "See, if my slave is the only one left, then why on Earth do I need you anymore?" He nodded once, and his men followed his actions. "I'd say that it's been a pleasure but it hasn't at all."

"Don't you bloody dare!" yelled Dane. He marched right up to Marlon, seemingly oblivious to the three pistols following his movements. "Think about this for a moment, you stupid fatty fool!" He glared at Branch. "If she is the last one, then where did he come from?"

Branch giggled before nodding a couple of times.

"Don't you get it? He is a chimera, a hybrid. One of his parents must have been just like her!" he announced while pointing at his slave.

"Yeah, you got me, fellas. My mum was a giant too." He winked at Marlon's slave. "Weren't a pretty a you, though. Still, I should be glad it weren't the other way around. Not that would have been a bit of a tight squeeze out!"

"No, don't tell them!" shouted the slave. "You can't do it."

Marlon watched this exchange with interest. Despite her silly protests, he was going to tell him exactly what happened to his mother. He had no choice. Marlon swung the pistol until he had her head within his sights. "You can shut up!" he screamed.

Marlon yelped out in pain when Branch suddenly snatched the pistol out of his hand.

"No use for any more threats to the pretty lady from you," he said. Branch tucked the gun into the back of his trousers. "I'll take you to her, and her pals, if that's what you want." He giggled. "But only if you really want this."

CHAPTER ELEVEN

Dane stayed silent while the group traversed through this ancient city. This decision was purely out of respect for the giant woman. That childhood snapshot helped him to mentally reconstruct these gutted buildings, to restore them to their former glory. He would have given his right leg to have been able to walk down these glorious boulevards, to gaze at the magnificent buildings at either side, to watch the children as tall as him climb those strange trees, to smell all the alien spices as well as gawp in amazement at the energy source high above him which made life under the ground possible in the first place.

It must have been paradise.

He couldn't imagine the pain that the giant must be in right now. This was her home. She had experienced all those delights. Dane took a deep breath. She had also suddenly found herself utterly alone in a deserted and dead city.

Nelson had found something next to the corner of one of the ruined buildings. He brushed away the dust before handing it the Dane. The old man had just discovered the probable reason as to why nothing down here remained intact. Dane rolled the bronze spear tip in his fingers before handing it back to the old man.

How had she reacted when she saw all those little people running riot through her city and stealing anything that wasn't nailed down? The image of the Inca smashing up this beautiful city didn't really sit right with Dane. After all, it's exactly what the Europeans had just done to them. Spaniards though, he knew they wouldn't have hesitated. The thought of finding a Nephilim city under the earth must have really messed with their heads, but it wouldn't have been strong enough to ransack it, hunting for gold.

She would have hidden away, obviously.

Branch came to a sudden stop next to a blank, grey wall. The giant pushed her way through the guards who tried to stop her. She grabbed the front of the hybrid's jacket and warned him not to do this. He paused for a moment before shaking her off while giggling.

"We have to do this," he replied. Branch's fingers danced along the side of the wall and a section slid away. "Yeah, we so have to do this. Come on, fellas, this is going to be so much fun!"

Dane had no choice but to follow them inside. Unlike the giant, he couldn't casually brush away the other men as if they were nothing more than puppies.

The last person shuffled inside and the door clanged shut, plunging them into absolute darkness. Branch released a dark chuckle. "Oh don't start crying just yet, fellas. The lights will come on in a second."

Just as he promised, harsh white lights above them flickered into existence, showing Dane what looked like some kind of ornate citadel that would have looked more at home in a Bosch painting than amongst a bunch of peace-loving gentle giants. He stared in disbelief at the brutal depictions of every inhuman act of atrocity he could think of to inflict upon another human. He found it impossible to look away from the beheading, stabbing, strangling as well as a whole host of other vile acts.

"Jesus!" spluttered Nelson. "This is like something out of a horror movie. What is this place?"

A three-foot wall encircled the middle of the circular room. Dane leaned over. The walls sloped towards a five-foot hole in the middle. It felt like they were standing on the edge of a huge funnel. There was no indication to where that hole led. He was getting a very bad feeling about their immediate future, especially with total disappearance of the outer door. Dane couldn't even see a joint.

Somebody brushed past Dane.

"Get ready to jump," whispered Bradley. "They'll be showing their hands any second now."

"What the hell is this place?"

Branch grinned at Nelson. "This is where the bad ones live." He put his hands behind his back. "Down there is where I was born."

Bradley tapped Dane on the shoulder and nodded over at

Marlon. That nutter had another gun, and he was pointing it straight at Benedict! He dived on the man and pushed him to the floor just as the world exploded in gunshot. He kept his hand on the back of Benedict's head and peeked over the top of the wall. There were three of them firing at each other now. How come none of them had hit each other?

Nelson, the giant, and the native girl had all got the same idea to drop to the floor. Bradley knew that it wouldn't take long before one of those maniacs started shooting the ones hiding behind the wall. He also knew that there was only one way out of here.

The decision to move came when Bradley stopped firing. He threw the pistol at Marlon before planting himself to the floor. Before Dane could push Benedict over the wall, incredibly, the giant slammed herself into Branch. His body hit Marlon. The giant then jumped over the wall and slid down the steep slope. Dane managed to get the two protesting men over the edge. He pulled their fingers off the edge of the wall and followed them. Dane turned his head to see Bradley right behind him.

Before he dropped into the hole in the middle, Branch started to shriek. The ear-piercing noise frightened him far more than what lay ahead. The noise abruptly cut off once Dane slipped through the hole. He gulped back his own scream when a bright blue sky suddenly filled his vision. Not that it would have made much difference, as the others under him had already found their own voices.

Dane had no time to wonder how they could have possibly fallen up as the ground raced towards him at an incredible rate. He uttered a silent prayer and…

…he crashed into a thick, dense bed of tightly-packed brown grass as soft as cotton. The stuff absorbed all his velocity. Dane lay close to the ground, unable to believe that he hadn't broken a single bone. He slowly sat up and looked around him. The others were close by and judging from their expressions, they too couldn't believe that they had reached the ground unharmed.

"We should find some shelter," said the giant. "They will have probably heard our noises." She looked straight at Dane. "You do not want to be here if they do show up. I'm so sorry about this. I truly am."

It took Dane a moment to realise that she wasn't talking about Marlon, Branch, or any of those idiots they had left behind. "Are you guys all okay?" Both Benedict and Nelson nodded. Bradley checked himself before standing up then grunted. The only one not to acknowledge Dane was the tribal woman. She had curled up into a ball.

He got up and hurried over to her. "It's okay now. You're safe. The others have all gone." He glanced across at the giant who looked close to following this woman's example and seriously wondered just how safe they really were.

His body and senses all told him that they were all back on the surface, yet, his mind and eyes both refuted that. It didn't matter how hard they tried to convince him of otherwise, Dane knew that they did not fall up.

"We should have stayed, Dane, and chosen the bullet." The woman finally moved her arms and lifted her head. Her eyes darted from him to the giant and back. "It would have been a good clean death. They are going to find us and chew on our bones."

Nelson and Benedict joined him.

"This is outstanding," said Benedict. "It's another level!" He looked up towards the sky. "That must be another fusion generator. I can't even begin to imagine the technology involved to create such a device."

"So why is this one working when the other one isn't?" Nelson looked at the giant. "And why does that question fill me with dread?"

The giant walked over to the men, leaned over, and picked up the woman. "Because to deactivate their energy source would be a monstrous act," she replied. "This woman is correct. They will eat you."

"We can't stay here," said Bradley. "Regardless whether this level is inhabited, Marlon and his goons are going to be following us, and they have guns."

Dane nodded. "He's right. We need to go."

"Go where?" Benedict threw up his arms. "Don't you get it yet? There is nowhere to bloody go. We can't get back home now, that's for sure."

"You don't know that."

"Of course I do, Dane," he snapped. "Have you not worked it out yet? This is their prison. Branch was on the ball when he said that this was where they put the bad people." He glared at the giant. "Jesus, can you imagine the exact opposite of her? Oh God. This place is where Jack's beanstalk took him!"

"Will you just shut up!" Dane so wanted to slap him.

"Only it wasn't the blood of Englishmen they first smelled," muttered Nelson. "This is why nobody knew about the giants. What's betting that the Spanish Conquistadors ended up down here as well?"

Dane shook his head. "Unlikely. For a start, how could they have possibly opened that section of wall?"

The giant started to weep. She took a deep breath. "I opened it, then waited until they we all inside before I shut them in."

"This is all very dramatic and everything, but can confession time not wait until we're no longer out in the open?" Bradley paused. "Bollocks, it's too late now. I think we have company. Look over there."

Dane followed his pointed finger. He couldn't see anything, then he caught movement. His heart started to race at the sight of a large pair of eyes looking right at them. The tree cover partially hid the rest of their body. "So much for going in that direction," he said. The leaves parted and Dane slowly lowered himself and motioned the others to the same when it stepped out into the open. "Jesus, look at the size of it."

The terror bird's malevolent gaze scanned the grassland. Dane silently wished it would decide that nobody was here and bugger off back into that woodland. It had to be twice the size of those monsters in the labyrinth. It was easily twelve feet in height. This had to be the biggest joke of the decade. To think that moments ago, they were thinking that a bunch of evil giant men would be running them down before grinding their bones to make bread or some such nonsense.

The monster's head stopped moving. It was looking straight at them. It squawked once. The terror bird obviously knew that they were all hiding in the tall grass.

"Shoot it, for crying out loud, Bradley."

"What with, my finger?" He glared at Benedict. "Idiot."

Dane just wished they would all shut up. He moaned silently when the woman wrestled herself out of the giant's grip. She firmly pushed the giant's hands away before she started to slowly walk towards the huge terror bird. "Come back here!" he hissed. "That thing will kill you."

She shook her head. "No, it won't," she replied, turning her head. "I know how to handle them. How do you think I was able to traverse through the labyrinth unharmed? Do not worry. I will send the bird away."

She walked through the shoulder-high grass, not looking back. Dane watched in fascination as the huge terror took one step towards the woman before it cocked its head to the side. If it wasn't for the fact that he knew just how deadly that thing was, he might have found its actions comical.

The giant got to her feet. She wrapped her fingers around Nelson's wrist and pulled the man over to Dane and the other two. "We must go now," she whispered.

"Wait, we can't leave her."

The giant sighed. "Yes, Benedict. We must. If we do not go now, then we will all die. The bird's companions will have heard its calling."

Dane flinched when the bird covered the distance between it and the woman in one pounce. It hammered its beak into the top of her head. He spun around, feeling his guts turn over. Jesus, what a way to die. Surely, that woman couldn't have possibly known the creature would do that?

"She wanted a clean death," uttered the giant.

CHAPTER TWELVE

He finally believed that he'd managed to get his heart rate, pulse, and headache under control. The flight from that huge bird and its five friends who'd run out of the trees to share the feast was the worst moment of his life; far worse than the spider incident. Nelson wrapped his arms around his jacket and pushed his back into the corner of the wall in a vain attempt to keep warm. The sun or fusion reactor, or whatever the hell it was, reduced its energy output and dimmed to a dull grey light about half an hour ago. He suspected that the drop in temperature was the real reason why his fear had now settled to a dull ache

The other four sat opposite him. None of those appeared to be cold, and they certainly hadn't noticed his discomfort. They were too entranced in the giant's story to pay him any attention. The archaeologist in him found her story of their great separation utterly fascinating. How could he not? These people had dispensed with their bad apples by simply throwing them down here. Benedict ought to be grateful that these people had chosen this path all those millennia ago. An advanced nation of giants, who weren't just a bunch of frightened sheep, certainly wouldn't have scurried underground when their smaller, uppity, primitive cousins knocked on their door.

Benedict looked up at that fusion sun, imagining just how much energy was stored in that device to enable it to power this huge cavern for all that time. He shivered, this time not from the cold. In the wrong hands, that thing could have the explosive capacity to make their largest nuclear weapon look like a bloody firework.

The maniacs, currently threatening each other with nuclear war would give their back teeth to own something so destructive. He tried to imagine how their world would be like if the opposing governments put all their energies into solving the world's problems instead of creating weapons that could vaporise their planet.

Could that huge, meek, soft-spoken woman be the future for their own kind? Now there was a scary thought. If the human race did follow a similar path to these giants, then he predicted that the species wouldn't last more than a century before going extinct.

"Guys, I know this is all interesting stuff, but do you think, by any chance that perhaps we should be devoting our time to looking for a way out of here? If, that is, there is one."

"We will, Nelson," said Dane. "Once there is enough light to see. None of us know what could be waiting out there."

"Apart from huge carnivorous birds," muttered Benedict.

"As for finding, don't worry, there's bound to be some way. After all, Branch must have found a route to the surface."

"For crying out loud, Dane. That freak of nature spent the entire time in our company lying to us. We don't really know that he originated down here. Come on, man, you're supposed to be a scientist. Look at all the available facts. The woman has already told us that she led the little people down here, and they sure as hell didn't leave. And what about the giants who are already down here? Don't you think that in all those thousands of years, just one of them might have found some way to leave?"

If Benedict's glare could kill, then he'd be dead by now, but Nelson didn't care. It was time that they all learned the truth of their dire situation. "To cap it all, you all heard what Bradley said about what he thought Branch was attempting." The giant joined Benedict in the staring contest, only she looked as though she was about to cry again. The bodyguard had already stated that he believed that the hybrid was going to throw them all down here with the exception of the giant. As far as he was concerned, that made escape from here impossible.

"Right, so you're going to lie down, roll over, and admit defeat?" Bradley got to his feet. "Your problem is that you overthink the situation. You all do. Has it not occurred to you that the reason why there's been no incursion from down here to her domain is because none of them wanted to leave?"

"That's just stupid," said Benedict. "What happened to the need to explore and to learn?"

Bradley shrugged. "Christ knows." He looked at the giant. "Perhaps all that was spliced out of them at the same time."

Nelson shook his head. "Of course I'm not going to lie down and admit defeat. That's what her kind did four hundred years ago."

"What happened to you, Nelson?" Dane leaned forward. "You never used to be this negative."

"All I'm saying is that we should accept the possibility that we might not get out of here, that's all."

"That's bollocks." Bradley leaped to his feet. "You're telling us, not bloody suggesting, that we're all going to die down here. You're showing your half-baked, stupid-ass idea down our throats and you expect us all to sit here and take it."

Nelson stood. "How dare you talk to me like that." He faced the bodyguard. "I'm not scared of you, young man. Hell, you've been on my bloody case for ages now. It's almost as if you have forgotten your place."

"Sit down!"

"Don't you tell me what to do."

Bradley dropped the stick he'd been holding and leapt on Nelson. He fastened his hand over the man's mouth and forced him back onto the floor. "Shut up, you moron," he hissed. The bodyguard looked up at the others. "We're no longer alone."

The man rolled off him, grabbed his stick, and pulled Benedict and the giant over to Nelson. "Stay here, don't move, and keep quiet." Both Dane and Bradley ran over to the other side of the wall before turning the corner, leaving them alone.

He was about to announce that those idiots were jumping at shadows when the shadow cast by the stone wall on the other side grew by a full foot. Nelson pushed his back against Benedict, hardly daring to breathe while listening to his heart rate, once more, go through the roof. The sound of a snapped twig reached his ears, and he inadvertently released a quiet moan when that shadow became longer. He moaned again when he spotted what looked like four thick, pale cream fingers reach around the edge of the wall.

Bradley couldn't believe it. Those fools had gone the wrong bloody way! Those fingers turned into a hand before the owner of that limb slowly peered around the edge of the wall. Nelson heard another moan, but it didn't come from him this time.

Nelson couldn't even open his mouth to make any sound. The appearance of this creature had utterly froze his body. What the bloody hell was he looking at? The figure…was it a boy?…now scuttled, like a huge crab into the open. Nelson knew that if he stood, instead of moving about on all fours, he'd be easily seven foot. Powerful muscles rippled under the black-and-white striped paint.

It took a moment for Nelson to realise that this creature wore a close-fitting mask. The inside of his stomach shifted. Oh no, this creature wore the dead skin of another creature like himself! Nelson's bowels loosened when the creature moved closer and allowed another of his kind to openly stare at them. This one looked identical to the first one, only he wore no mask. It was just a child, no more than eleven or twelve.

Even with the fact that their new guests were only kids, he was still frozen solid. The sheer size of them, as well as their terrifying appearance and movement, did nothing to quell his terror.

"We don't mean you any harm," said the woman behind him. Her soft tones brought back the realisation that he didn't face this first contact alone, and although the giant's reassuring voice helped to calm him down, it seemed to have the opposite effect on the two boys. They both acted like they'd just been electrocuted.

"What are we going to do?" he said, looking over to where the over two had gone. What the hell were they doing back there? Hell, could Bradley and Dane not see the trouble they were in? Nelson turned his attention back to their visitors, almost crying out as the pair of them each took a filthy hand off the ground in order to reach behind their back to pull out thin curved blades as long as their bodies.

The one in the mask then opened his mouth and barked out a collection of sounds in what Nelson presumed to be their language. The boy repeated the same words, but this time, Nelson caught the unmistakable air of impatience and malice threaded throughout that last sentence.

"How are we supposed to answer you when we can't speak your language?" Benedict stood. He took one step forwards.

"Look, don't you guys have any grownups we can speak to?" He looked back at Nelson and smiled. "Hey, don't look so worried, my man. They're probably more scared of us than the other way around. I remember this time, back in the middle of the Congolese forests, facing a tribe of kids very much like these two when—"

The old man didn't have a chance to continue as both boys let out a single screech, which sounded unnervingly like that terror bird before they jumped on Benedict, bringing the struggling man to the ground. Nelson jumped to his feet and ran at them only for the woman to throw her arms in his way, effectively clotheslining the man. Nelson tried to get up, but she planted her foot on his chest. "Get off me, you bitch!" he screamed. "Bradley! Dane! Get back here, get back here now!"

He managed to lift his head, only to watch the two boys jump off the now still Benedict and scuttle away. She took her foot away, allowing Nelson to move. He jumped up and ran over to his friend. He placed his fingers on the side of his neck. He couldn't find a pulse. "You bitch!" he snarled, turning his head. "You let them kill him!"

The giant dropped down beside Nelson and wrapped her arms around his body. He so wanted to push her away, but he didn't want to lose her warmth and comfort. "No, Nelson. I did not let them. Your friend was already dead before he hit the ground. Look at the blade cuts down your friend's chest. They weren't deep enough to kill him."

"Jesus." He looked up into her face. "Poison?"

"This is a dangerous world, Nelson, and if these boys hunt the birds, then it makes sense to use every advantage at your disposal. If you had intervened, then I fear that you too would be lying beside your dead friend."

He felt an incredible sense of loss when the giant did release him. She stood, dipped her head when she walked past Benedict's body, then walked over to the edge of the wall. "It is okay now, Nelson. They have both left us."

He found it almost impossible to contain the emotions now running riot through his system. He looked over at Benedict and wanted to weep, yet, when he shifted his attention to the giant, a different set of emotions travelled through him. After all, despite the size disparity and the huge age gap, she was still very beautiful. He wanted her to hug him again, which made him even more upset as well as guilty for allowing his base feeling to try and rule him.

"What about the others?" he said, standing. Nelson dipped his head, just like she did, and hurried over to the other side of the wall. He felt so angry with them for leaving them almost defenceless. If it hadn't been for the woman, he could have died as well.

He put his hand on the top of the wall and scanned the dark horizon. Nelson couldn't see anything out there. This didn't surprise him in the least, considering their light source now looked like a very dim light bulb a hundred miles in the sky. He sighed heavily while wondering how to place his dreadful encounter into the possible history of this place.

It felt so inconsiderate, as well as ill-mannered, to engage his academic mind in the light of recent events. Right now, it helped to keep the bubbling insanity at bay. Christ, so much for regaining his clarity. It's obvious that the gas Marlon used on him had not dissipated at all.

Their appearance and behaviour suggested that those boys came from a primitive society and yet this wall, although ancient, was created using tools made from hard alloys. He tapped the rock; this stuff was granite. Had their society regressed?

That did make sense. After all, if you leave a group of volatile people alone in a confined area for any period of time, there was going to be conflict. For the first time since been dumped in here, this news actually made Nelson feel a little better. After all, if would explain why the giants down here hadn't found a way to escape. They were too busy fighting each other. It also might suggest that their numbers were very low, meaning that Benedict might be the last of their group to die.

His musing came to an abrupt end when he picked out two figures racing towards them. He heard their indistinct shouts at the same time at a dozen flickering lights suddenly illuminated the treeline. "Oh crap!" he shouted. That was torchlight. The giant appeared beside him.

"We need to go."

"Oh, you think?" The two men were now within sight. Blood poured down Bradley's face. He looked behind them, counting thirty torches.

Dane reached them, he took one look at Benedict. "Oh no, not him." The archaeologist closed his eyes for a second. "How many were there?"

"Two of them." Nelson put his hand on the man's arm. "I'm so sorry, dude."

"Two against a full tribe." He glanced over his shoulder. "Like we have a choice!" Dane waited until Bradley caught up with them before pointing to the right. "We go that way."

"What? That's the way we came. It's where those birds are!"

Bradley nodded. "Exactly why those behind us won't follow." He set off running. "Unless you want to say here?"

Nelson took one last look at the silent army running towards them before racing after the others. That dread of never seeing the real sun again had returned, and he didn't think he'd be able to shift it this time.

CHAPTER THIRTEEN

It took the freak precisely eight seconds to make up his mind. He then spent the next two minutes promising Marlon everything from enough gold to sink a continent to an army of giant warriors the likes of which had never been seen before. He said that he knew who to talk to in the underworld, that he had influence with every warring tribe, that they'd all be willing to trade with him for the right kind of goods.

Marlon allowed the freak to continue his rambling speech for a further couple of minutes before ordering his remaining three men to pull their blades away from his naked body. Was the freak begging for his life, basically saying anything just to get Marlon's associates to stop prodding him with their shiny blades? Of course he was, and exactly how many lies had he just spun? That too, Marlon knew would be many. Yet, within that intricate web of lies, he also knew spun a few threads of truth, and he intended to push through all that bullshit in order to find them.

Branch might be a serial liar, but even his lies did contain a shred of truth. That much, he had already discovered.

"You know what, Branch? I like you. No, I do. See, just like you, I've had my share of adversity. I believe this is the sole reason as to why I have turned out to be rather dangerously unstable." He leaned back against the circular wall and watched his other companions for a moment. The four remaining employees must be going out of their minds about now. Despite Marlon's instructions to cut the freak, Branch had still refused to open that door.

He knew just how frustrated the others were becoming and ached for Marlon to order them to cut off a piece of the freak. It wouldn't matter how much they tortured Branch, he wouldn't give up the secret of the door. Of course he wouldn't, for as soon as he relinquished his only hold on them, he'd be a dead man.

Marlon respected that. It showed him that this ungodly creature had known much hardship, so much so that resilience was now part of his very being. He picked up the hybrid's castoff clothes and passed them to the shivering man. "Here, put them back on."

He waited until the freak had covered up most of his dignity before continuing. "It must have been tough for you, my friend. I'm guessing that the others cast you out at an early age. Comparing you to my slave, I can understand why, Branch. It isn't easy, being different, not knowing love and having to fend for yourself."

The hybrid stared down at Marlon, his unreadable expression telling him far more than any of his previous outbursts under torture.

"I am sure that some of what you said to us earlier was true, Branch." He clicked his fingers twice. One of his associates approached him. "Open your backpack." The man did as instructed. Marlon pulled out the last of their supplies and gave half of them to Branch. "Go on, eat. I assure you they're not poisoned or anything."

The others were more than a little pissed at him giving their supposed prisoner half the food, but they wouldn't dare say anything. They'd trust his strategy. Marlon frowned. Then again, what if they didn't? They were all tooled up. Sure, their guns were all empty, but at least they possessed knives. What would he do if they did mutiny? Hit them with his shoe?

"I am willing to strike a deal with you, Branch. All I ask is that you introduce us to someone who will be able to furnish me with a few giant warriors. If you do that, I will give you the slave with my blessing. Does that sound like a good deal?"

"Wait, you mean we're all going down there?"

Marlon glared at backpack man, noting the knife in his hand. "It was the plan."

"But, how will we be able to get back?"

Marlon approached the man. He gently placed his hands on his shoulders. "My friend," he said, smiling. Marlon felt the man relax, then snatched the large knife out of his hand. Maintaining eye contact, he flipped the knife and plunged the blade deep into the man's stomach. "Consider this the termination of your contract." Marlon sawed across his waist before pulling the knife out. He pulled off the backpack before allowing the man to fall to the floor.

"I'm sorry you had to witness that," he said to the other two while staring in fascination as the moaning man on the floor tried in vain to stop his steaming insides from spilling out. "Events are in a state of constant flux, meaning that to achieve your goal it is sometimes necessary to switch alliances." He finally looked up. "You two, at this present time, are no use to me. Branch will be my guide, and for that, he will be rewarded. Now, you have a choice. You stay here or," Marlon climbed onto the wall, "you join us in the greatest adventure of your lives." He gazed back at the squirming man. He had lost his private agonising battle to stop his insides from leaving his body. "He will be dead in hours, perhaps sooner." He smiled at the two men. "This means that they'll be enough food to last you for at least three, maybe four days."

Branch quietly laughed. It was good to hear the hybrid's sense of humour returned. It proved to Marlon that he was right about his resilience. He motioned the men to climb onto the wall. "Up you get, chaps."

"You really are sick," one of them spurted.

Marlon shrugged. "Perhaps, or perhaps I am just driven? Look, it is not like we can't return. Branch here is the living proof that it isn't a one-way journey."

As soon as they joined Marlon on the wall, Branch ran forward and pushed them. Marlon shared the hybrid's laughter as the pair of them screamed all the way down the funnel until they dropped through the centre.

"You really will give me the slave?"

"Of course, I will, my friend. I don't go back on a deal."

Branch slowly nodded. He climbed onto the wall, paused, then jumped back.

"What are you doing?"

The hybrid picked up the body, then threw it over the wall. Unlike the other two, he didn't make a single noise as he slid down.

"We're going to need him," he said. "There's worse things

down there than the other giants. Believe me, I know this."

"Yeah, I already guessed that much, that's why I made sure we took the other two with us as well."

Branch giggled. "You know something, I think I'm beginning to like you."

Marlon shifted a little to the side to avoid the man's blood streak which now stained the surface. He waited for Branch to start his journey into the unknown before he jumped forward.

There was a brief experience of weightlessness before he found soft fur-like plantstuff caressing his body. The hybrid's large green eyes filled his vision. He heard human voices as well as cries and howls from unknown sources. He suddenly remembered Branch's last-minute warning and desperately searched around where he had fallen for the knife. Where was it? The bloody thing had to be around here somewhere. Marlon almost screamed out in surprise when Branch pulled him onto his feet.

"You dropped this," he said, giving Marlon the knife.

"My God! We're inside another cavern." Even though shadow covered the land, Marlon could still pick out distant features of hills, woodland beyond this plain of tall grass-like material. He turned his attention back to the two men who sat crossed legged opposite each other, looking thoroughly miserable. "Are you not going to look beyond your own tragedy at where we are? This is so magnificent!"

They shook their heads.

"Some people just aren't happy. You could be back up there, looking forward to tucking into a portion of dead human."

"That's still a possibility. I've already had a bloody look around, and I didn't see any cafes close by."

Marlon wanted to stab him in his face. How dare he try to put a downer on his current euphoria. Thankfully for the man, he was too excited and giddy to exact revenge. Instead of berating Mr. Grumpytrousers, he drank in the glorious sight of those distant trees again. What delights awaited them beyond this grass? He couldn't wait until it got light. Marlon's optimistic dreaming shuddered to a halt. "Branch, it won't stay dark like this, will it?"

The hybrid shook his head. "No, it'll get light in a few hours. By then, we'll have found ourselves in a safer place than this." He walked towards the two sitting men, giggling when they both cried out. He reached behind them and lifted the body, giggling again when bits of the body's insides fell on their heads.

"May I use your knife, Marlon?"

He gleefully handed his prized possession to the hybrid when the men's expressions switched from disgust to dread. Was he about to butcher them? Marlon would even allow him to do the deed. After all, this was his territory now. They were all fragile dolls in the freak's deformed hands.

Branch skillfully cut away the dead man's clothing before jointing and dismembering the corpse. It brought back the realisation that this creature had the strength of half a dozen men. He dissected that man as if it was no more than a two-day-old cooked chicken carcass.

"The last time I was in this area, there were two tribes fighting for territory. Thing is, there's a huge colony of birds who hunt the small animals who live in the grass. Thankfully, the birds only hunt in the light, and the two tribes usually come out at dusk and dawn." Branch twisted off the other foot and chucked the limb high into the air.

"So why are you doing that?"

He grinned while winking at Marlon. "See, this is why I like you. The questions you ask usually make sense. See, this grass is inedible. Nothing down here can eat the stuff. So, see if you can guess what the animals which race through this stuff at high speeds like to eat." The hybrid shivered. "They look a bit like wild boar, they do. They don't make a single noise. The nasty little bastards sneak up on you." Branch pulled off the man's head then dropped it into the lap of the only man still sitting down, before handing the knife back to Marlon.

Branch threw the mutilated corpse over his shoulder then walked past Marlon. He nodded over at the other two men. "It's best you two keep up with us. You really don't want to stay in this place, fellas. The animals don't normally attack adult humans. Too big, you see. It hasn't stopped them from carrying off any kid stupid enough to venture into these fields once it got dark." He stopped and turned around. "And right now, that is exactly what you would look like to those vicious buggers."

Marlon couldn't help but chuckle at that. Despite the few setbacks, this adventure really was beginning to get exciting. He so wanted to ask Branch a thousand questions about this place, now believing that the hybrid would be less likely to lie all the time. Why should he lie? After all, the hybrid now thought that he was in control, that he was the expedition leader. This didn't really bother Marlon as he knew the real score. What did bother him was asking a dozen questions which would make him sound like some eager little schoolboy, asking the teacher for answers while the rest of the class sniggered behind his back.

"When did you last come by here?" Marlon dare not ask anything else.

The hybrid shrugged. "Not since I was a boy. Not that it mattered. This place isn't as large as it looks, and news down here travels fast. If there had been a change in the status quo then believe me, I would know. Of course, as it's been years and years since I've been down here, stuff might have changed already." He glared at Marlon. "I mean, it's not like I've been staying in contact with any of the bastards who wanted to eat me, you know?" The hybrid tutted loudly before continuing to push his way through the shoulder-high grass.

Marlon stopped and allowed the two men to pass him. It was best that he should bring up the rear. This way if the hybrid came out with another smart answer, he wouldn't end up stabbing him in the back in a fit of temper.

CHAPTER FOURTEEN

Dane heard Nelson muttering some incomprehensible words. He wasn't sure if they were directed at him nor did he care. The insanity of their current surroundings, as well as the possibility of an ambush, took up all his concentration.

Of all the buildings to stumble across down here, the last place Dane expected to find was a church. Oh, no normal church either. He swallowed down bile as they walked past yet another gutted giant nailed to the wall. He forced himself to look at the poor man, and allowed his analytical mind to visually examine the corpse. It wasn't what he wanted to do, but the more he learned from their evidence, the better prepared he would be. If that was even possible.

Judging from the advanced state of decay, their new friend had been in that position for a good few months. Did that mean that this place wasn't used daily? How much of a relief would it be to rest up, knowing that in the next pretend dawn, they'd all open their eyes without finding metal bolts pushed through their limbs while their steaming insides slopped onto the filthy floor? Don't forget to mention the small animals tearing off the toes.

He took a deep breath, determined not to allow that 'I'm never getting out of here alive' mind-set to sink its pervasive claws into his over-tired mind. Dane glanced over at Nelson, stumbling after him, the older man's face a picture of terror. He was already in the bad place. Dane doubted whether poor Nelson would ever be the same again, if they all did make it through this nightmare.

"I hope they fired the decorator," murmured Bradley. He stooped, picked up a bone piece, and casually flung it at the rotting corpse.

"Jesus, have some respect, will you?"

Bradley just shrugged.

"He does have a point, Bradley." Dane stopped walking and gazed steadily at the bodyguard, hoping the man would pick up the hint. "Best we try to behave ourselves, just in case. After all, we could be here for a few hours."

"You're shitting me!" gasped Nelson. "We can't stay inside this vile place!"

Bradley coughed. "Why not? It's protected from the elements. It's warm, and the creatures outside don't come in here."

"How can you possibly know that?

"Obvious," replied Bradley. "Those corpses wouldn't be hanging on the walls, that's how I know."

He listened to the pair of them having a go at each other. It wasn't exactly what he had in mind, but at least Bradley's wind-up routine kept Nelson's mind away from the threat of death. Dane moved past them, his footsteps crunching over the tiny pieces of bone.

Bradley's idea had paid off. None of the giants followed them, and thankfully, they didn't run into any more of those evil birds.

He caught up with the giant who hadn't moved away from what appeared to be some kind of altar. She looked worse than Nelson. "How are you holding up?"

"What do you think?"

"Sorry. This must be so hard for you."

The giant lifted a thick book from the surface of a triangular-shaped altar and dropped it on the floor. Clouds of dust catapulted into the air. "Such a vile distortion of everything," she spat. "This building, everything inside it is devoted to the worship of death and yet…" she lifted the cover with her toe, "and yet, although I expected to find this, it isn't as monstrous as I believed it would be."

Dane wasn't too sure that he heard that right. "It can't get any worse, can it? I mean, look around you. This is just horrible, like something out of a maniac's nightmare."

"That I agree with, Dane, but it is not recent. None of this is new." She pushed the book to the side. "From what I can make out, that is some kind of log, a record of who they have sacrificed in this place. None of these poor souls are in here."

"Forgive me for being sceptical here, but how could you possibly know that?

"As fantastic as it is, the marking of time is still the same as the old way, Dane. They might not have become sloppy with their record keeping but not with marking down the dates. According to that book, in human terms, several years have passed since they last sacrificed an unbeliever to their God."

"So this is, or at least was, a church of some kind. You give me the impression that this place isn't frequented too often then?"

"We can only hope."

"Then let's see if we can find somewhere to hole up that isn't so unpleasant."

The giant smiled at him. "That would be nice, Dane."

He walked back over to the others and found, to his annoyance, that they were still in a heated debate. "Guys can we lessen the noise now? Let's see if this church has a room with beds, a kettle, and perhaps even a TV?"

"Dane, will you please explain to this meathead why we can't stay in this filthy place?"

"Can you believe that he wants us all to leave and sleep somewhere else?"

He closed his eyes for a second. "Come on, man. This is the safest place we've found. You saw those huge birds. Who knows what else could be hiding in the dark."

"This is an evil place. Can't you feel it?"

"Seriously." Bradley turned away, looking disgusted.

"Do you remember the lost catacombs we found in Crete? Remember how both of us needed to get the hell out of there because of the atmosphere?"

"A maze in Crete?" said Bradley. "You mean the one with the bull?"

"It was a Minotaur, actually."

Dane knew exactly what he meant. They were the first humans down in that cold place for over three thousand years, and yet they still felt the evil clinging to the very stones. He too was aware of the amount of suffering and death that had happened in here. Dane also knew that the knowledge that more victims would finish their existence tortured to death, made the experience even more difficult to comprehend. In Nelson's overactive imagination, he saw that long-dead Minotaur stalking him through that maze, one more step bringing certain doom.

"That's just a stupid story," said Bradley. "It didn't really happen."

"We found its bones."

Dane nodded. "Yeah, we did." He glanced over at the giant and frowned. She looked drunk. That wasn't a good sign.

"Right, head of a bull, body of a human? You're pulling my leg. Stuff like that never existed."

Nelson's overactive imagination was liable to get all of them killed. "I feel it too, Nelson. Of course I do, but there's nothing else we can do. We are out of options here."

The bodyguard nodded. He bent down and picked up another bone piece. "Listen to the man, Nelson. We are stuck here. At least for the moment."

He looked down at where Bradley had moved the bones. "That's weird," he said, dropping down to the floor. He picked up a couple of the larger pieces and threw them to the side, then used the edge of his hand to push away the small pieces. Dane lowered his head and blew away the dust to reveal part of a thick red line painted over the stone floor. "Can you see that, Nelson? There's a pattern under here. I wonder what it means."

Dane looked over at the giant, meaning to ask if she knew, but one look at the woman told him they had more important things to worry about. She was in real trouble now. He got to his feet only for Bradley to knock him back down.

"We're no longer alone. We have to hide!"

His heart raced at the sight of the new shadows forming in front of the door which they first entered. They had seconds to find some cover. The female looked as though she was having a seizure. What the hell was wrong with her? "We can't leave her!" Dane ran over to the woman, gratified to see the other men had joined him. He grabbed her left arm while Bradley took hold of the woman's other arm. They managed to pull her twitching body between a row of wooden seats. Thankfully, the noise the intruders made walking on those bone shards disguised the noise they created while pulling the woman into a corner.

The woman's eyelids fluttered before snapping open. Dane could tell straight away that she still wasn't with them. "Come on, sweetheart! Come back home." The giant opened her mouth wide. Dane slammed both his hands over that huge mouth. "Please, don't scream. You get us all killed." Finally, her eyes focussed. She blinked once before managing to nod slightly.

The giant removed Dane's hand but kept hold of one of them. "I'm okay now," she whispered. "I'm sorry. I am not sure what just happened."

"It's okay." Dane heard Nelson gasp. He shifted his head to the left. "Bloody hell!" Giant warriors were entering the building from three different entrances. The type which ended Benedict's life had walked through the same large open doorway as they did. These weren't the kids described to him by Bradley and Nelson.

The sheer size of these men took some getting used to. The female amongst them was big enough, but the three giants now approaching that alter were at least another two feet taller. He truly felt like a gazelle hiding from a pride of lions. They were anatomically similar to them. The exceptions being their arms were a little out of proportion to their bodies, and they still retained a slight brow, a possible throwback from their early hominid ancestors. It was a puzzle as to how the female looked more human than they did.

The three giants, painted like zebras, were not the only group to enter this unholy building. From two different doorways, Dane watched another group of painted warriors approach the first group. It was obvious from the outset that the new group was from a different tribe; they chose a selection of greens and brown to cover their huge bodies. He would have chuckled at their posturing if it hadn't been for the painful reminder that their hands were large enough to cover his head and probably possessed the strength to crush it like an over-ripe pear.

The last group was the only one not painted, they also wore clothing fashioned from bird pelt. The other two quietened down once the last group reached their side of that alter. It then occurred to Dane that those floor lines had to be territory markers, and this place was a neutral meeting place. Whether or not this was its original purpose was another question entirely.

When the giants began to converse, the female released his hand. She started to shake. "Are you okay?" he hissed.

She nodded again. "Yes. Sorry, just hearing them brought back painful memories. I will be okay."

He turned back and strained his ears, trying to listen to their language. It was unlike anything that he had ever heard before. He looked back at Nelson, who shrugged back. Dane was about to ask the female when all their voices silenced. The atmosphere grew heavy. The giants looked at each other before they gazed at the doorways.

Another group of giants were framed in the doorways. The first group fell to their knees and began to hum, while the new arrivals slowly made their way towards the alter. Each group contained three giants. They were all smaller, about the same size as the female, and none of them wore body paint. Deep red material covered their torsos. Were these some kind of priest or shaman? All nine of them met in the middle. They linked hands, then thrust their hands back and let loose a series of ear-deafening howls.

It was the most frightening sound that he had ever heard. Looking at the others, he saw it hadn't just affected him. Both men now looked uncomfortable, but not as bad as the female. While they howled, she twisted and bucked. She looked to be in real pain. She was going to give them away!

He put his hands over her ears. It calmed her down a little, but she wouldn't stop trembling. "We have to get her out of here," he said above the noise.

Bradley nodded. He turned around and ran along the edge of the wall for a couple of metres. He stopped beside a break in the stone before returning. "There's a narrow tunnel just over there. If she breathes in, she might just fit through."

"What if she doesn't?"

Dane so wanted to slap Nelson. "We have no choice. Come on, let's get out of here!"

They managed to pull the woman up to the wall when their howling suddenly changed to match the humming coming from the other giants. He lifted his head a little higher to see if he could tell what had changed. As soon as he saw the arrival of two more figures, Dane now wished that he'd kept his head down. He knew exactly what was going to happen next. There was a single priest stood on the threshold, and he held the end of a thick rope. The priest gave it a savage pull. From behind the outer wall, Dane watched in horror as a smaller figure stumbled into the doorway and fell in front of the laughing priest.

The giant casually pulled on the rope, lifting the struggling man onto his feet. From where he lay, it looked like the priest had captured a human, and Dane guessed that's exactly what this ceremony must symbolise. Although the priest towered over the prisoner, the bound man was still well over seven foot.

One of the nine original priests approached the newcomer and forced the rusted head gear belonging to a Spanish conquistador onto the prisoner's head. The room went deathly silent. The new priest released a single howl before all priests took out short curved blades and fell on the prisoner.

Nelson moaned loudly. Dane's heart raced when the largest giant in the feathered group jerked his head in their direction. Dane threw himself down, but it wasn't good enough. Through a crack in the wood, while his companions fed, he slowly made his way through his feasting companions, towards them.

"Go!" he urged. "Get out of here!" He waited until Nelson and Bradley had left before helping the giant up. "Can you do this?"

She nodded. "Yes, I think so." The female glanced behind her. "Go, Dane. Run. I'm right behind you."

He followed the other two into the tunnel, fully aware that the giant must have seen their escape, and after witnessing what these savages did to people of their kind, Dane didn't want to hang around. The tunnel stunk of death. He held his nose while splashing through the black water, eager to catch up to the other two. He just hoped that this foul-smelling tunnel wouldn't lead them to a dead end.

Something resembling a severed torso floated past his ankles. He stopped and choked back a scream. Dane then realised that he could only hear the feet of Nelson and Bradley splashing through the water. He turned around and saw the giant at the beginning of the tunnel. "Come on!"

She shook her head. "No, I can't leave." She quickly looked behind before turning back. "You need to listen to me," she said urgently. "Head east. Oh Dane, there's so much I wanted to tell you. I'm so sorry. There is a way out of here. Look for a forest of dark red leaves. Now go!"

He watched her pull something from inside her clothing. She unfolded the object. It was a mask made from what looked like skin. The other giant was now visible. Dane waited until the female placed the mask over her face and went over to the giant before Dane turned around and ran towards the others. Dane hated himself for leaving her, but he knew that he had no other choice. If any of those giants saw him or the others, they wouldn't last another five minutes.

CHAPTER FIFTEEN

Marlon wasn't sure if he'd ever been more disappointed. He had now seen his first group of giants, and they weren't that much larger than her slave. What upset him more than anything was they cringed when they passed the group. They actually cringed! The phrase gentle giants sprang to mind. They were farmers, not warriors.

This even beat the current record of when his father and brother gave him an Action Man for a Christmas present. Only when he opened the box, the bastards had forced an old Barbie doll inside. To make the moment complete, they had only dressed the doll in miniature versions of his favourite clothes. They had thought their prank to be hilarious.

He could feel his temper rising again. That bloody freak had lied to him yet again, and this had to be the biggest lie of all. Not only were the giants punier than he expected, it was obvious from the amount of acknowledgements she'd been getting from these farmers, Branch had been here recently. In fact, Marlon believed the freak was a frequent visitor to this place.

They were travelling along a dirt road, heading towards a collection of scruffy-looking buildings. It wasn't exactly a thriving metropolis or a fortified town full of huge, angry armour-plated warriors that Branch had promised him. More giant farmers worked in the fields at either side. It wasn't the same stuff that they'd fallen in. He guessed that this stuff was their equivalent to wheat or barley, only this stuff was bright yellow and smelled similar to cinnamon.

Branch looked up. He stopped and bowed his head. "We have company heading towards us, fellas! For my example, get your eyes looking at the bloody dirt."

The freak was spot on; there were some more giants heading down the path. Perhaps he had been a bit too premature in his first assessment of these giants as these new ones were significantly larger than the farmers. He didn't bow his head. Marlon wouldn't submit for anyone, no matter who they were.

Branch muttered to himself while rifling through his pockets. He pulled out a number of random objects, like a can of coke, a small bottle of vodka, and a tiger ornament. It then hit Marlon that this guy was a trader. He even took off his boots. Why had Marlon not worked this out before? This is how the freak had managed to stay alive for all this time.

This looked more promising. These four guys actually did look intimidating. Three of them were painted in black-and-white stripes, while the giant at the back wore a red outfit which looked like a T-shirt and shorts combination. Marlon sniggered. Did this clown know how stupid he looked? The freak must have heard the noise as he turned his head, and saw that Marlon hadn't obeyed his command. He spun around, covered the distance between them in one stride, and slapped Marlon around the back of the head. The blow threw him into the dust.

"I told you to bow for your masters," he thundered.

Marlon stayed where he lay while listening to Branch converse with the giant dressed in red in some strange language. He interspersed lots of bowing with the dialogue. He had no clue to the content, but from the body language coming from the pair of them, the giant in red was the master here.

There was more a great deal more shouting before they shook hands. The silence didn't last longer than a couple of moments. The ground under his cheek rumbled. Marlon dared a quick peek and saw a pig-like animal the size of a horse pulling a crudely assembled four-wheeled wooden cart holding two metal oblong cages. Branch pointed at one of the other associates. He grinned then pointed at Marlon before shaking his head and pointed at the remaining associate. The other giants picked up the sobbing men and threw them into the cages.

Another giant, one who looked more like one of the farmers, patted the animal's shoulder. It turned around and headed back towards the village, with the others following on. Branch grabbed

Marlon's shoulder and dragged him to his feet. "I've just saved your life, Marlon. You can thank me later." He chuckled again. "If there is a later." The freak shook him. "You listen to me, human. Where we are going, tame humans are not allowed in the settlement without a collar. You just better be good."

Marlon managed to nod without punching the arrogant goon right in the nose.

They reached the outskirts of the village minutes later. Two giants of the larger variety opened the gates to let the inside the compound. Marlon stopped wondering how to start convincing the more fearsome giants to join his new army when he saw just how many humans were wandering around the village. Branch was correct: all the tame humans did wear collars. He also saw that every one of them had limbs missing. They were all very thin and dirty. He got the feeling that the giants treated them worse than animals.

Branch grabbed his shoulder again and pulled Marlon through the compound. He tried to attract the attention of the other humans, but every one acted like he wasn't even there. Marlon only stopped when Branch dug his fingers into Marlon's flesh.

"Do you know why they have no arms and legs?"

Marlon shook his head.

"Take a guess." Branch chuckled. "Yum, yum, yum."

The possession ground to a halt. The four giants lifted the two cages onto a wooden platform and placed a few metres apart. Marlon watched, fascinated, while two priests climbed onto the platform. They bowed their heads and muttered some nonsensical sentence before they each approached the corner of a cage.

They pulled out a small metal wheel and pushed it onto a rod, half-way up the cage, then they started to twist the wheel clockwise. The crowd in front of Marlon all leaned forward. None of them spoke, not that Marlon would have heard anything as the two men in those two cages were doing enough screaming, shouting, and begging to drown out every other sound. Their pleas for mercy obviously fell on deaf ears as they didn't stop twisting their wheels.

They weren't just begging to be set free. The wheels were bringing two of the cage sides closer together. Each turn wiped out another inch of space. The priests were smiling; they looked like they revelled in the humans' discomfort.

By now, both men were having difficulty in talking due to the steel wire mesh cutting into their flesh. The priests continued to turn the wheels for another few seconds before stopping. They walked over to the edge of the platform and raised their arms. At this gesture, the crowd went wild. Two more priests approached the edge of the platform and passed the priest a sword each.

"You better watch this next bit closely," said Branch. "This is what will happen to you next if you don't behave."

The priest walked back to the cages. They pressed the blade against the mesh, muttered another chant, then lowered the blade, slicing through the skin and tissue pushing through the gaps in the metal.

Both men shrieked in agony, much to the amusement of the assembled villagers. The priests picked the little square parcels of flesh from the platform and threw them to the villagers before returning to the wheels.

Marlon's throat tightened when some more priests lifted another cage onto the platform. "Please don't tell me that's for me!"

Branch slapped him again. "You're big for a human, but you're not that big. You really can be stupid.'

'I'm not stupid,' he growled. "I'm not scared of you or your friends. You'll find this out if you hit me again." Satisfied that he had made his point, he turned to watch the priest push another giant into the cage. This one wore the remains of clothing made from bird skin. It seemed like such a waste. Their prisoner had the build of a warrior. He would have made a great addition to his army.

"Branch. You need to tell the leader that I need to speak to them."

His companion giggled. "That's not going to happen, fella."

Marlon pressed a thick blade against the hybrid's back. "You're going to do as you're told or you'll end up dead."

"I can't. It isn't allowed. They'll kill the pair of us."

"You're going to die right now if you don't."

He expected some resistance. It was only natural. "You'll be dead right now if you don't open your ugly gob and do as you're told." Marlon very nearly slid in the blade when the freak opened his mouth and uttered a stream of words in the giant's language. One of the giants responded in kind before pointing at Marlon while laughing.

Branch shook his head. "They said food isn't supposed to talk back."

Marlon grinned. "How little they know." He reached behind and pulled out his hidden pistol. "Let the games begin." Marlon aimed at the prisoner and fired one shot. He didn't even need to look to know that is round had just blown out the back of the giant's head. He guessed the dead giant would have preferred a quick death to what awaited him. Over a dozen giants now surrounded him, each one holding a spear thicker than his wrist. Marlon guessed he had their attention now.

He placed the gun on the floor and raised his hands. "Branch, you tell them that they can have more weapons just like that one to use against their enemies if they help me destroy my enemies."

Branch spoke again. This time, the giant didn't laugh once he had finished. This time, they smiled.

The giant replied with just two words. Marlon didn't need a translator to understand that the giant would do anything to possess such awesome firepower. Of course, he wasn't going to hold up his part of the bargain. These giants were too untrustworthy. They'd rather eat humans than fight for them. It would be a lot safer to kill most of them. Keep a couple of the larger specimens and set up a breeding program. This was just great. Everything was working out perfectly.

CHAPTER SIXTEEN

The distant cloud of dust that briefly appeared on the horizon had long gone, but the apparent disappearance of their pursuers hadn't convinced Dane that the bastards were still following them. After all, there couldn't be that many places for three fugitives to run to, and the ones after them would know this landscape like the back of their hands. Nelson had told him to stop worrying, that whoever had been following them were long gone.

Even Dane didn't think the older man believed what he was saying. Nelson would probably say anything as long as it was the exact opposite of Dane's opinion.

The childish moron blamed him for losing the female, like she fell out of his pocket or something. If he didn't know better, then he would believe that the idiot had fallen in love with her. At one time, that idea sounded utterly preposterous. Nelson only loved his work. Nothing else mattered. However, the man's mind wasn't as it used to be, and something had happened to Nelson on this journey which had sent the old man a little strange. Still, it's nothing a good holiday wouldn't be able to fix. Even though Nelson's attitude had annoyed the hell out of him, this adventure had certainly awoken something inside Dane's body that he thought had gone out years ago.

"They're back, Dane," said Bradley. "No shock there."

Now that Bradley had confirmed Dane's suspicions, Nelson's high and mighty attitude went right down the toilet. He changed in an instant from being openly sceptical to utterly terrified. Dane now wished Bradley had kept his silence. At least in the former state, Nelson carried on walking.

"You can't stay there, man."

Nelson had sat himself down on a small boulder.

"Sulking is only going to you killed."

"I'm not sulking," he spat. "I'm just resting, while trying to work out a way out of here."

"We already have one of those," replied Dane.

"Oh yeah? I guess this involves walking through this stupid woodland until it gets too dark to see before we all lie down and wait to get eaten by the wildlife? Come on, admit it, Dane. We're lost, and we've all been walking around in circles for the last two bloody hours. Oh wait. No, scratch the wildlife option. Trooper Joe here has just informed us that the giants are back on our tail so perhaps we're all going to spend a lovely night getting nailed to a wall?"

"Have you quite finished?"

Nelson shrugged. "Look, just go. Go on, leave here like you did with our large friend."

"Fine by me," said Bradley. "Your whining was beginning to get on my tits anyway." The bodyguard nodded at Dane before turning around and walking away.

Dane gave Nelson a smart salute. "Look on the bright side. As we're going around in a circle, we'll probably see you again in about ten minutes. Unless the giants don't get you first. If that does happen, we'll send a commiseration card to your family. We'll punch a few holes in it with a pencil first, just to make it realistic." Dane spun around. "Be seeing you."

"You evil bastard," whispered Bradley, once he'd caught up.

"Yeah, well, he deserved it. The old man needs to come to his senses and to stop acting like a child."

"Perhaps. I think there's something else, something that can't be attributed to his frequent hissy fits."

Dane stopped. "What do you mean by that?"

He responded with his infuriating shrug. "I'm just saying that he would benefit from professional medical help."

"Fine, once we're clear of this, we'll get the old man checked." He glanced up and saw the man in question had started to come to his senses.

"Keep this to yourself," whispered Bradley. "He's unstable enough already."

"I'm not saying anything. It would break the poor man."

"That's what I mean."

"You misunderstand, Bradley. It would break the daft bastard to learn that you really care about him."

Dane shook his head. He waited for Nelson to reach them before setting off again. True to form, Nelson still said they were probably going around in circles. Privately, Dane did have the same fear, as the path he followed certainly did not follow a straight line. He slowed down before stopping. Dane crouched and ran his fingers other the plants in front of him. Someone had been here in the last few days. "Bradley, here's a question. If you walked backwards down a beach until you reached the sea, then retraced your steps coming back, how would it look like to someone else?"

It took his a few seconds to answer. "That someone just came out of the water?"

Dane grinned. "Exactly right!" He turned to the old man. "Nelson, you're a genius! Come on, chaps," he said, purposely stepping off the path. Instead of following the path, he kept in a straight line, aiming for what felt like the most unlikely direction to take.

To his left, he watched the path wind up and down, like a huge snake. Dane ensured he stayed with his own shadow on the right of him. After a few more minutes, the path vanished from view. Dane also noticed that the light had started to fade. He knew from last night, it wouldn't take long to get dark.

"I think I see a change," said Bradley.

"It's just the path."

Bradley shook his head. "That's on the other side, Nelson. There," he said. Pointing between two large trees. "The air is shimmering."

Dane pushed past the bodyguard, entranced by the vision. "I can see it too. It's like looking through a curtain of hot air." He walked right up to it, paused, then slowly pushed his right arm through the shimmering curtain of air. He counted to five. No excruciating pain savaged his arm so he took that as a good sign. Dane gave Nelson another mock salute before taking a deep breath and stepping forward.

"You have got to be joking!" he gasped, staring in wonder at what the screen hid from view. "The stairway to heaven," he whispered before turning his head. The others were running towards him, but it was obvious that they still couldn't see beyond that screen.

"It's a pyramid!" said Nelson. "A great big, sodding pyramid in the middle of the woods." He began to laugh. "Now why does this not shock me?"

"The steps are not that high. It won't be that difficult to reach the top."

Dane silently agreed with Bradley and this worried him. It seemed a little too easy. He walked a little closer and examined the stones. It wasn't the most ornate pyramid he had examined, but he guessed it wasn't put here to be admired. The style looked more like the structures in Egypt rather than anything constructed on this continent. He then reminded himself that he stood inside the earth rather on it.

There wasn't any sign of weathering. Odd considering how long he believed this thing had been here. Then again, as far as he knew, the giants upstairs might have made this shortly before committing mass suicide. Dane had no way of checking. The only change to the grey stones was right at the top where he saw several red trees clinging to the surface. Ingenious. From the outside of the woods, it would look like an extension of this woodland. The perfect camouflage.

Despite his eagerness to get out of this vile place, Dane couldn't bring himself to take another step towards the structure. His cynicism had just demanded to know why none of the giants living here had tried to leave. Even his earlier story of them having everything they needed down here failed to wash. It's not like this place was all that difficult to find either. Hell, if they could locate a hundred foot stone structure in the middle of woodland, he was sure that at least one of those giants must have stumbled across it in all those thousands of years. In fact, one of them had done it. The female giant obviously knew of its existence.

He took another step closer to the base.

"Oh, that's not great," said Bradley. "It looks like our friends have entered the woods."

"So? They won't know where we are. We're surrounded by an

invisible screen, remember?"

"Doesn't mean they won't be able to home in on your big gob, Nelson." Bradley watched them move towards a large tree then stop. He looked at Dane. "Their presence concerns me. Thousands of years have passed, and yet none of those giants have left this place. Why do you think that is?"

"Not sure. It's what I've been asking myself as well. It boils down to two answers. They can't leave or they won't." He took another step and almost lost his balance as the ground shifted. "What the hell?" He lifted his leg and saw that he'd just stood on some bones. Dane crouched and carefully pushed away the loose vegetation.

There were thousands of bones under the leaf litter. Looking at the type of plant growing over this stuff, he imagined that these bones went all the way to the base of the structure. In fact, it wouldn't surprise him if the bone bed surrounded the pyramid. Now that he was closer, he could pick out a few tiny pieces resting on the stones.

"So, now we know," murmured Nelson.

He had realised that the older archaeologist had joined him. Then again, why was he even surprised? Nelson could smell bones from a mile away. He now knelt on the floor with both his hands picking up pieces of bone, dropping them then picking up a few more.

"What do we know, Nelson?" It did please Dane to see that Nelson had relaxed slightly. The old man was in his element. He also had a captive audience. Why wouldn't he relax? This is what Nelson lived for.

"Notice how there's no scratch marks on any of the bones? Also, they're all whole. No splinters." He picked up a large tibia. "This is remarkable. A quite recent specimen, perhaps less than a few months. I'd also suggest that the rest of the skeleton will be in that lot."

"The only thing I knew that could do that are piranhas, and I severely doubt that they're responsible."

Nelson chuckled. "You're not that far from the mark there. Not a bad guess for a meathead."

"Insects?"

"That's my guess."

"So, if we start climbing, there's a chance we might get eaten alive by a swarm of flesh-eating beetles?"

"Nelson, are you sure about this? I know some forensic scientists use beetles to strip the flesh from bodies, but they have to be dead already and the process can take days. From the distance these bones have fallen, the victims have died in seconds."

"The bones don't lie, Dane. You know that."

"We have no other choice," replied Bradley. "It looks like the giants have found their courage and…" he growled. "Branch is with them, and so is Marlon. Shit, why can't that bastard do the decent thing and die already?"

"Now we know why all the bones are covered up. This must be how Branch leaves this world." Dane walked across the pit, cringing at the sound his boots made when they crunched down on the bones. He reached the base and climbed up onto the first step. "If Nelson is right, then we should all keep our eyes peeled once we get about halfway up." He continued to climb, painfully aware that the other two were right behind him, doing their hardest to climb faster than he was. He turned around and saw the reason for their haste. The others were now stood at the edge of the bone pit, all watching their progress in silence. It felt like they were simply waiting for one of them to release the beetles, or spiders, or whatever lay hidden behind one of these stones.

That illusion was shattered when Marlon pulled out a pistol. "Shit." Dane climbed a lot faster, not really caring where he put his hands anymore. A round smacked into a stone just above his head.

"Come back down here right now or I'll shoot you off." The man at the base of the pyramid chuckled. "It makes no difference to me. Hell, forget what I just said, you three keep climbing. I'll just carry on shooting, it's all fine by me."

"What are we going to do now?" Nelson looked at Dane. "We can't go back down. They'll eat us. I don't want to be eaten!"

Dane looked behind him and saw Marlon getting ready to take another shot. The giants that towered over the fat man obviously thought this was hysterical. Even Branch was grinning like a loon. He looked over at Bradley, then paused. "Push the stone beside your left hand. See if moves."

"Have you gone mad?" cried Nelson. "What if the beetles come out?"

"Rock and a hard place," muttered Bradley.

"Then we die. At least it'll be over in seconds instead of days." He watched the bodyguard try to push the stone with no effect. Bradley then climbed up another metre and jumped on it.

The stone sank into the surrounding area. Dane felt a vibration followed by the noise of scratching. Nelson cried out when swarms of black bugs rushed from the hole and spread in all directions across the stones. "Put your hands over your ears!" he shouted. "Close your mouth and your ears." He did the same then leaned his body against the stone, and when he felt their tiny legs and bodies reach his legs and started to crawl up his clothing, Dane did the one thing that he promised himself he'd never do again.

He prayed.

The prayer lasted precisely three seconds before he started to scream inside as the vile creatures scurried through his hair, over his eyelids, and along the back of his neck. The torment felt like it was lasting hours until, finally, the creatures all dropped off his body. Dane counted to five before he dared to open his eyes. The bugs were now moving as one towards the base of the structure. The giants, as well as their guests, had already fled.

"How could you possibly know they wouldn't eat us?"

"They've been engineered, Nelson. Just like the spiders,"

"And the birds," added Bradley.

"Come on, they're coming back already. We need to get out of here." Dane shivered once, remembering how it felt to have all those horrible little things crawling all over him before he started to climb. Within seconds, Dane was almost at the peak. He looked down and moaned when he saw the giants were now right at the base. The evil bastard had simply sacrificed two of their men to appease the bugs. The insects had already gone to ground. Marlon, Branch, as well as two of the giants, began to climb the pyramid. Marlon saw him looking down. He stopped, raised his gun again, and fired.

This time, he didn't miss. Dane ground his teeth as the round slammed through his upper arm and ricocheted off the stone behind him. It didn't matter though as they had already reached the top. He watched Nelson stand and raise his hands. His fists touched the ceiling, changing the azure to a flicker of over a dozen rainbow colours.

"We've done it!"

"Good job, fellas!" shouted Branch. "You've got the door, but you still need a key to open it." He laughed. "Oh, that was fun. Now it's over, and you're basically burger meat."

Marlon pointed the pistol at Dane's forehead. "Look, I've got nothing against you, or any of you for that matter. Let's all go back down, and we'll see if there a deal we can make?"

Dane sighed heavily before he stepped down the stones. He stopped opposite Marlon. "You want a deal, fat boy?" He clenched his fist tight and swung it straight into Marlon's shocked mouth. His gun went flying, and Marlon rolled all the way down the stone structure, screaming.

"You vicious, nasty human," snarled Branch. He reached over and wrapped both his huge hands around Dane's neck and started to squeeze. There was nothing he could do; Dane kicked and bucked but nothing took away the constant pressure. His world went to monochrome. He was going to die. Dane shut his eyes, not wanting that grinning monster's face to be his last ever image.

The roaring in his ears vanished at the same time as the pressure on his throat. Dane began to cough. He managed to open his eyes. Both Nelson and Bradley held his arms. He tried to speak, but all that left his burning throat was a single croak.

"Look down there," suggested Bradley.

He did as the man said and saw that Branch sat on the floor with the rocking Marlon next to him. There were a large amount of giants surrounding them, but these all wore feathered cloaks. He saw one of the giants walk to the front and wave.

The female had returned. Bradley lifted him to his feet. "Can you talk yet?"

"A little," he managed to say.

"Go thank her for all of us." Bradley reached behind and pulled out something very familiar.

"The artefact!"

Bradley grinned. "Yeah, I lifted it from Branch ages ago. I

reckoned it would come in useful."

Dane made his way down the steps, towards the smiling female.

"I'm sorry that we could not arrive much sooner. It appeared that my new mate had other ideas." She gently stroked his head. "Take care of yourself, Dane. Please, do not give away our presence. Can you do that?"

He nodded. "Don't worry, nobody is going to find out. I'll make sure of that."

"Thank you. We shall keep these two here." She pulled her large mate over. "These people need my guidance. The evil which once lingered here died out many years ago. What we saw in that church was just a watered-down remnant of some half-forgotten ritual. They will now have enlightenment, Dane. I will help to purify the bloodline." She bent down and kissed him on the forehead. "Now go. Go back to your people."

He thanked her then climbed the stones, towards his waiting friends. They had cut a hole into the roof of the cavern. He would make sure that his part of the bargain was kept. Would he see her or their kind again? Somehow, he doubted it. The giants went through their extinction event and only just clung onto existence. The daily TV news reports continued to show that the two superpowers were at each other's throats. Somehow, Dane didn't think that once the nuclear missiles started flying, their species would not live through their extinction event.

THE END

www.ingramcontent.com/pod-product-compliance
Lightning Source LLC
Chambersburg PA
CBHW051957170626
46808CB00007B/2657